INSTRUCTIONS FOR DANCING

INSTRUCTIONS FOR DANCING

nicola yoon

Delacorte Press

Text copyright © 2021 by Nicola Yoon
Jacket art copyright © 2021 by Renike
Jacket lettering copyright © 2021 by Jyotirmayee Patra

All rights reserved. Published in the United States by Delacorte Press, an imprint
of Random House Children's Books, a division of Penguin Random House LLC, New York.

Delacorte Press is a registered trademark and the colophon is a trademark
of Penguin Random House LLC.

Grateful acknowledgment is made to Bank Robber Music for permission to reprint an excerpt from
"The Book of Love," written by Stephin Merritt, published by Rough Trade Publishing
by arrangement with Bank Robber Music. Used by permission of Bank Robber Music.
All rights reserved.

GetUnderlined.com

Educators and librarians, for a variety of teaching tools,
visit us at RHTeachersLibrarians.com

Library of Congress Cataloging-in-Publication Data
Names: Yoon, Nicola, author.
Title: Instructions for dancing / Nicola Yoon.
Description: First edition. | New York : Delacorte Press, [2021] |
Audience: Ages 12 and up. | Summary: "After picking up a book from the library, Yvette—who has
given up on love—gains the ability to see how other people's romantic relationships will end"—
Provided by publisher.
Identifiers: LCCN 2020026948 (print) | LCCN 2020026949 (ebook) | ISBN 978-1-5247-1896-1
(hardcover) | ISBN 978-1-5247-1897-8 (library binding) | ISBN 978-1-5247-1898-5 (ebook)
Subjects: CYAC: Love—Fiction. | Dating (Social customs)—Fiction. | Divorce—Fiction. |
Ability—Fiction. | Books—Fiction. | African Americans—Fiction.
Classification: LCC PZ7.1.Y66 In 2021 (print) | LCC PZ7.1.Y66 (ebook) | DDC [Fic]—dc23

The text of this book is set in 12-point Adobe Garamond.
Interior design by Ken Crossland

Printed in the United States of America
10 9 8 7 6 5 4 3 2 1
First Edition

For my mom,
who is still smiling despite it all.

And for my father-in-law,
who smiled through it all.

CONTENTS

The book of love is long and boring

No one can lift the damn thing

It's full of charts and facts and figures

And instructions for dancing

But I

I love it when you read to me

And you

You can read me anything

—The Magnetic Fields, "The Book of Love"

Almost nobody gets out of love alive.

—Helen Fisher

CHAPTER 1

A Better Version of Me

BOOKS DON'T WORK their magic on me anymore. It used to be that if I was in a funk or in the barren hinterland between sad and mad, I could just pluck any random one from my favorites shelf and settle into my fuzzy pink chair for a good read. By chapter three—chapter four at the very latest—I'd be feeling better.

These days, though, the books are nothing but letters arranged into correctly spelled words, arranged into grammatically correct sentences and well-structured paragraphs and thematically cohesive chapters. They're no longer magical and transporting.

In a past life I was a librarian, so my books are arranged by genre. Until I started giving them away, the Contemporary Romance section was the biggest. My favorite of all time is *Cupcakes and Kisses.* I pull it down from my shelf and flip through it, giving it one last shot to be magical. The best scene is when the no-nonsense head chef and the sexy, constantly brooding line cook with the mysterious past have a food fight in the kitchen. They both end up covered in flour and icing. There's kissing and a lot of dessert-related wordplay:

Sugar lips.

Sweet buns.

Sticky situations.

Six months ago this scene would have made me gooey inside. (See what I did there?)

Now, though? Nothing.

And since the words haven't changed from the last time I read them, I have to admit the problem isn't the book.

The problem is me.

I close the book and stack it on top of the others I'm giving away. One last trip to the library tomorrow and all my romances will be gone.

Just as I start putting them in my backpack, Mom pokes her head into my room. Her eyes travel a circuit from my face, down to the tower of books, up to the four empty rows on my shelf, and then back to my face.

She frowns and looks like she wants to say something, but then she doesn't. Instead, she stretches out her hand and pushes her phone toward me. "It's your father," she says.

I shake my head so hard my braids whip around my face.

She jabs the phone my way again. "Take it. Take it," she mouths.

"No, no, no," I mouth back.

I've never seen two mimes arguing, but I imagine it would look something like this.

She moves out of the doorway and all the way into my room. I have just enough space to dart around her, so I do. I sprint down our small hallway and lock myself in the bathroom.

Mom's inevitable knock comes ten seconds later.

I open the door.

She looks at me and sighs.

I sigh back at her.

Most of our communication these days comes in the form of these small exhalations. Hers are Frustrated and Long Suffering and Exasperated and Impatient and Disappointed.

Mine are Confused.

"Yvette Antoinette Thomas," she says. "How long are you going to keep this up?"

The answer to her question—and I think it's a fair one—is forever.

Forever is how long I'm going to be angry at Dad.

Really, the better question is: Why isn't she?

She slips the phone back into her apron pocket. There's a dusting of flour on her forehead and some in her short Afro, making it look like she suddenly went gray.

"You giving away more books?" she asks.

I nod.

"You used to love them," she says. The way she says it, you'd think I was setting them on fire instead of donating them to the library.

I meet her eyes. It feels like maybe we're having a moment. If she's willing to talk about me giving away my books, then maybe she's willing to talk about something real, like Dad and the divorce and how things have been since.

"Mom—" I begin.

But she shifts her eyes from mine, wipes her hands down the front of her apron and interrupts me. "Danica and I are going to make brownies," she says. "Come down and help us."

The baking's new. She started the day Dad moved out of our old house, and she hasn't stopped since. If she's not on shift at the hospital, she's baking.

"I'm meeting Martin and Sophie and Cassidy tonight. We're supposed to start planning our road trip."

"You spend more time out of the house than in it these days," she says.

I never know what to do when she says something like that. It's not a question and not an accusation, but it has a little bit of both in it. Instead of answering, I stare at her apron. It reads *Kiss the Cook* and has a drawing of two enormous red lips smacking.

It's true that I'm not home much these days. The thought of spending the next few hours baking with her and my sister, Danica, fills me not with despair exactly, but something close to it. Danica will be dressed perfectly for the occasion—a vintage-style apron with a matching chef's hat that sits in the middle of her Afro poufs. She'll talk about her latest boyfriend, who she is (very) excited about. Mom will tell gory emergency room stories and insist on playing reggae music, something old-school like Peter Tosh or Jimmy Cliff. Or—if Danica gets her way—they'll play trip-hop while Danica documents the whole thing for social media. They'll both pretend that everything is just completely okay with our family.

Everything is not okay.

Mom sighs again and rubs her forehead. The flour dust spreads.

"There's flour," I say, reaching to wipe it away.

She dodges my hand. "Leave it. It's just going to keep getting dirty anyway." Mom's originally from Jamaica. She moved here when she was fourteen with Grandma and Grandpa. The only time she has a Jamaican accent is when she's nervous or upset. Right now her accent is slight, but it's there.

She turns and goes back downstairs.

As I get dressed, I try not to think about our not-quite-an-argument but end up thinking about it anyway. Why was she so upset with me for giving away the last of my romance books? It's like she's disappointed in me for not being the same person I was a year ago.

But of course I'm not the same person. How could I be? I wish I were as unaffected by the divorce as she and Danica are. I wish I could bake with them, carefree. I wish I could go back to being the girl who thought her parents, especially her dad, could do no wrong. To being the girl who hoped to have a love just like theirs when she grew up. I used to believe in happily-ever-afters because they had one.

I want to go back and unknow all the things I know now.

But you can't unknow things.

I can't unknow that Dad cheated on Mom.

I can't unknow that he left us all for another woman.

Mom misses the version of me that used to love those books.

I miss her too.

CHAPTER 2

(Former) Favorite Romance Genres

Contemporary

1. Enemies to Lovers—Asking the perennial question will they kill each other or will they kiss each other? I'm kidding. Of course they're going to kiss.

2. Love Triangle—Everyone loves to hate love triangles, but actually they're great. They exist so the main character can choose between different versions of themselves: who they used to be, and who they're still becoming. Side note: If you ever find yourself choosing between a vampire and a werewolf, choose the vampire. See #1 below for more on why you should (obviously) choose the vampire.

3. Second Chance—These days I realize this is the most unrealistic trope. If someone hurts you once, why would you give them the chance to do it again?

Paranormal

1. Vampires—They're sexy and will love you forever.
2. Angels—They have wings that they'll use to envelop you or to take you away from this place to wherever you need to be.
3. Shape-shifters—Jaguars and leopards mostly, but basically anything in the big cat family. I once tried reading about dinosaur shape-shifters. T. rexes, pteranodons, apatosauruses, etc. They are as horrifying as you think they are.

CHAPTER 3

Give a Book, Take a Book

BY THE TIME I get downstairs the next morning, Mom's already left for her shift at the hospital. Danica is at the dining table taking pictures of the brownies she and Mom made. They're arranged into a pyramid on one of Mom's fancy new cake platters. Danica is from the jaunty-angle school of picture taking. She tilts her phone and circles the brownie pyramid, taking picture after jaunty picture.

I get myself cereal and sit at the table next to her. We've been in this apartment for six months, but it still feels temporary, like I'm just visiting. I keep waiting to get back to my real life.

Compared to our old house, this place is small. I miss having our own private backyard. Now we share a courtyard with twelve other apartments. Our house had two bathrooms, but now we only have one. Mostly, though, I miss how every room held our memories.

Danica settles on a photo and slides her phone to me so I can see her post. "You can't even tell they're burnt," she says with pride.

She's right. They do look perfect. I scroll through her posts. There's a selfie of her and Mom dusted with flour, holding a big block of chocolate and laughing, that makes me wish I'd stayed and helped. I read through the hashtags—#motherdaughterbakenight #blackgirlmagicbaking #perfectbrowniesareperfect—before sliding the phone back to her.

"How come you're not at brunch?" she asks.

Usually I spend Sunday mornings with my best friends at Surf City Waffle, the absolute best waffle place in all of Los Angeles. This morning, though, they're all busy.

"Everyone's got stuff," I say.

"So you're just gonna hang around here, then?" she asks, and not in a way that makes me think she wants me to hang around here.

I drop my spoon back into the bowl and take a good look at her. Most days, she looks like a supermodel from the '70s with her enormous Afro, bright glittery makeup and vintage clothes.

Right now she looks even more beautiful than usual. If I had to guess, I'd say she has a date. But I don't have to guess, because the doorbell rings a second later. A huge smile breaks across her face, and she runs to the door with a squeal.

In the last year, Danica has had eight different boyfriends, which is an average of 0.667 boyfriends per month or 0.154 boyfriends per week. Anyway, my problem is not the quantity or even the quality of her boyfriends (to be clear, the quality could be better. I don't know why she chooses boys who are so much less interesting and smart than she is), it's the fact that she's dating at all. Why am I the only one who learned the lesson of Mom and Dad's divorce?

I leave my bowl on the table and try to sneak through the living room so I can avoid saying hello. No luck.

"Hey, Evie," says the guy. He says "hey" as if it has more than one syllable.

"Hi," I say back, trying to remember his name. He's dressed in board shorts and a sleeveless T-shirt, like he's going to the beach or just got back from it. He's white, tall and muscled, with long, messy blond hair. If he were furniture, he'd be a really nice-looking shag carpet.

We stand there awkwardly for a few seconds before Danica puts us all out of our misery. "Ben and I are thinking of going to the movies," she says. "You can come if you want."

But the look on both their faces tells me two things:

#1: They are not thinking of going to the movies. They are thinking of staying here. Alone. In the apartment. So they can make out.

and

#2: If they were going to the movies, they wouldn't want me tagging along.

Why did she even ask? Is she feeling sorry for me?

"Can't. Have fun, though," I say. The only thing I have to do today is go to the library and get rid of my books, but sharing that will make me feel pathetic. I go upstairs and get dressed.

When I leave, I say bye like it has more than just the one syllable.

I'm on my bicycle and halfway to the library when I remember that today is Sunday. My library is closed on Sundays.

Going back home right now while Danica and Ben are "hanging out" isn't really an option. It's one of those beautiful spring days when the morning fog lingers and the air smells wet and new. I decide to head to the park at La Brea Tar Pits, but with a detour through Hancock Park.

The Hancock Park neighborhood is only ten minutes from our apartment, but it might as well be another world. The houses here are as big as castles. All they're missing are moats, portcullises, dragons and damsels in distress. Every time we drive through here, Mom says it's a crime that houses like these exist in a city with so much homelessness. She treats a lot of those homeless people in the ER.

I ride slowly, meandering down street after street, gawking at the enormous, pristine lawns and the enormously expensive cars.

Eventually I find myself on a street lined on both sides by jasmine bushes and overgrown jacaranda trees. The branches overhang the street and form a canopy of purple petals. I feel like I'm riding through a tunnel into a fairy tale.

The sun slips behind a cloud, and the air is suddenly colder. I pull over onto the sidewalk and take my jacket from my backpack. As I'm about to ride off again, I spot one of those small wooden neighborhood library boxes. It's bright blue and looks like a miniature house with a gabled roof and weathered white doors that are latched shut. A small placard reads *Little Free Library*.

"You certainly have a lot of books for us, dear," says a woman just as I'm propping up my bike.

I scream and whip around. An old woman is standing behind me, not even a foot away.

"Holy fuckballs," I say, and then slap my hand over my mouth. "Sorry, I didn't mean to curse. I didn't see you there."

She chuckles at me and moves closer. Her skin is a pale and thin brown, like weathered paper.

"Never mind about the cursing," she says. "Though one wonders what a fuckball might be."

I smile but look past her. Where did she even come from?

"Is this your library?" I ask.

"Well, I made it, but of course it's for everyone. Do you know about these? The idea is to get people reading and actually talking to their neighbors instead of just living next door to them." She rubs her hands together. "Now, what do you have for us today?"

I swing my backpack to the ground and take out an armful of books.

She takes some from me and presses them close to her chest. "These are very well loved," she says, looking down at the titles. She's one of those people who mouths words as she reads. It makes it seem like she's chanting a weird spell. *Barely There; Cupcakes and Kisses; Destiny's Duke; Love, Set, Match; Tiger's Heart.*

"They're all great," I say. My voice comes out in a scratchy whisper. I clear my throat. "You should read them."

"Why are you giving them away?" she asks.

She's standing closer now, still clutching the books she took from me.

I grab more from my backpack and consider telling her the truth. That the books don't feel like they belong to me anymore. That love stories are like fairy tales: you're not meant to believe in them forever.

I stopped believing in them the day after Dad moved out.

It's funny how a day can start out just like any other and end up so different. Sometimes I wish there were a weather report for your life. *Tomorrow's forecast is for routine high school shenanigans in the morning, but with dramatic parental betrayal by late afternoon, ending with wild emotional despair by nightfall. Details after the next commercial break.*

I'd spent the day at school in shock, not quite believing that Dad wouldn't be there when I got home. By lunchtime I was sure I could convince him that he and Mom were making a mistake. After school, I took the city bus all the way to Santa Monica and then rode my bike across campus to the Humanities building, where his office is. I took the stairs two at a time, thinking about what I was going to say. Maybe the problem was he didn't realize how much Mom loved him. She isn't always the most demonstrative. Or maybe they needed some more non-parent time together, a weekly date night or something. Or to find a hobby to do together so they could "reconnect" in the way relationship experts always talk about.

I ran down the hall to his office, thinking he'd understand. We always understood each other.

I didn't knock on his door. I should've, but I didn't. I just opened it and burst inside, hoping he'd be there. He was there. And he was kissing a woman who wasn't Mom.

I looked back and forth between them. I tried to convince myself that maybe this relationship was new, that it'd only started in the last two days. But of course, that was silly. It wasn't a first kiss, and it wasn't a last one. This kiss said there was a whole history to their relationship. It was one of the many kisses that broke up our family and broke Mom's heart and broke mine too.

Dad ran his hand down his face. "Evie, sweetheart," he said. "You didn't knock."

I'm not sure if he was scolding me.

When he and Mom told us they were getting separated they said they'd just grown apart. That they still loved each other and loved us. But that was a lie. The reason Dad left us was right here, wearing a jade-green dress and big hoop earrings and pressing her hands to her lips like somehow it could make me unsee what I'd seen.

I backed away from them and ran through the door and down the hallway and down the stairs until I was outside. Dad called out to me, but what was there to say? There wasn't anything at all to say anymore.

That evening, Mom told me Dad had called and told her what happened. She said she was sorry I had to see that. She asked me not to tell Danica. She said she never wanted to discuss it again.

Of course, I don't tell the old woman any of that. Instead, I shove the last of my books into the little library. When I look

14

at her, she seems sympathetic, like somehow she heard all the things I didn't say.

I latch the door shut. "Well, have fun reading those," I say.

She points at the library. "Aren't you going to take a book, dear? The rules are 'give a book, take a book.'"

"There isn't one to take," I say.

"Are you sure? I'm certain someone left one earlier."

I reopen the door and spy the book she's talking about in the back left corner.

The book is called *Instructions for Dancing*. It's a slim paperback with water-damaged and dog-eared pages. Underneath the title there's a simple line drawing of two sets of footprints facing each other.

I flip through the pages reading chapter titles: "Salsa," "Bachata," "Waltz," "Tango," "Merengue," "East Coast Swing," "Lindy Hop." Each dance has its own sequence of numbered diagrams with arrows pointing from one set of footsteps to another.

"Maybe I should leave this for someone who wants to learn how to dance," I say, and start to put it back.

"That someone could be you, dear." She comes closer to me. "I insist," she says.

It seems so important to her that I take the book and drop it into my backpack. "Nice meeting you," I say as I hop onto my bike.

"You too," she says. "Take good care."

At the end of the block, I turn to wave goodbye.

But when I look back, she's no longer there.

I ride for two blocks before realizing that I'm heading east instead of west, toward home. How did I get so turned around? I pull off to the side of the road and check my phone. It's already after three. I've been meandering for four hours. My stomach growls, like it too just realized how late it is.

I take the nonscenic route home, pedaling fast while still being careful. LA drivers sometimes act as if bicyclists don't exist. I lock away my bike and turn the corner to my apartment. Danica and Ben are on the stoop. They're so busy staring into each other's eyes, they don't realize I'm only a few feet away.

There are some things you don't need to see in your life. Your little sister making out is one of those somethings. I'm about to clear my throat and spare us both the trauma. But before I can, she leans in and kisses him.

My vision goes black, like the moment just before a movie begins.

And I see.

CHAPTER 4

Danica and Ben

DANICA IN OUR school cafeteria. She's sitting at her usual table, surrounded by her friends. The cafeteria is bustling in the usual ways. Some kids are talking, eating, laughing. Some kids—the always-alone kids—are not talking, not laughing. Danica's ultrabright today in a fuchsia outfit that was probably once someone's prom dress.

From the right, a tray slides over and bumps into hers. Ben is on the other side of the tray, smiling.

"I was thinking about asking you out," he says.

"Don't you have a girlfriend?" Danica asks.

"Not anymore," he says, and leans in. "If I did ask you out, what would you say?"

She leans in too. "You actually have to ask to find out."

"Want to go out with me?"

"Sure," she says. "Why not?"

This moment right now, the two of them kissing on the stoop like no one can see them.

Danica on a beach at night surrounded by firepits, and the firepits themselves surrounded by her friends, who are partying or warming their hands and faces or just watching sparks fly up and away. She stumbles through the sand, away from all that. Her eyes are restless, searching. She walks past lifeguard station twenty-three and then twenty-four. At station twenty-seven, she finds Ben, but he's not alone. He's kissing his ex-girlfriend who, it turns out, isn't an ex after all.

Danica lying in bed in her room, alone. She scrolls through her social media, deleting photos and posts and comments. She changes her relationship status to Single. She unlikes and unfollows until there's no evidence to be found anywhere that she and Ben were ever together.

CHAPTER 5

The Bonfire

THE VISION ENDS and the real world comes back into focus. I'm back where I was, standing on the sidewalk outside my apartment.

Danica and Ben are still on the stoop, but they're no longer kissing. They're both gaping at me.

Ben looks confused.

Danica looks outraged. "What the hell, Evie?" she demands, and stomps down from the stairs. "Why are you staring at us like a creeper?"

She's right there in front of me, real enough to touch. Not a hallucination. But I can't shake the image of her in the cafeteria and at the beach bonfire and alone in her room erasing her history with Ben.

"I—what?" I say, feeling slightly dizzy.

I must sway or something, because she comes closer. Her expression changes from annoyed to worried. "Are you okay?"

"Yeah, I just . . . I don't know. That was the weirdest thing—"

"We should go inside," she says.

"I forgot to eat lunch," I say as she guides me into the apartment. "And then I rode really fast to get home."

She helps me over to the couch. "Maybe I should call Mom," she says.

That snaps me out of my daze. "No, don't," I say. "I don't want her to get worried. I just got a little woozy for a second."

She sits next to me and takes my hand. "Let me see your eyes," she says, sounding a little like Mom when she's in nurse mode.

I can't remember the last time we were this close physically. Looking at her face is a lot like looking at mine. We have the same warm brown complexion, the same high round cheeks, and the same full pink lips. Somehow, though, those features come together more dramatically on her. She looks like a supermodel. I look like the supermodel's pretty-but-less-attractive sister.

She turns my face from side to side. I have no idea what she's looking for.

We've never been the best-friends-forever kind of sisters, but we used to be closer than we are now. She honed most of her makeup skills by practicing on my face. I used to supply her with new romances to read (she loves them almost as much as I did) and bands to listen to. Back when I was still dating Dwayne—my first and only boyfriend—we even went on a couple of double dates.

She squeezes my hand and looks like she's about to say something, but Ben interrupts. "Yo, D, I gotta go. I have that thing."

Is that thing cheating on my sister with your ex-girlfriend?

I want to ask. Which is a ridiculous thing to want to ask, because he hasn't cheated on her. At least, I don't know if he has.

I pull my hand from Danica's and stand up. "I'm really fine."

She skips over to him and they slip out the door together.

I lean back into the couch cushions and rub my temples, still freaked out. Was it a hallucination? Can you get those from being too hungry and too tired and too emotional? Or maybe it was one of those vivid dreams you get sometimes just as you're waking up?

I've always had a good imagination, but that was more than good. It was cinematic.

My stomach reminds me that I'm hungry.

Danica comes into the kitchen just as I'm about to eat one of the brownies.

"If you want, some of us are going to the beach tonight for a bonfire," she says.

I almost drop the brownie. "You're going to the beach tonight?" The image of her stumbling through the sand looking for Ben and then finding him with someone else flashes through my mind. "Is Ben going with you?" I ask.

"Of course." She narrows her eyes at me. "What's the matter? Oh, let me guess, you don't like him."

"I didn't say that—"

"But that's what you mean."

That's not at all what I meant, but I don't know how to explain what I did mean. How do I tell her I had a strange vision and I'm afraid she's going to get her heart broken tonight?

"Whatever," she says. She spins away from me and takes off upstairs.

Later that night, I'm lying on the couch with my laptop and communing with the course catalog for NYU (New York University, where I'm going to college in the fall) when Danica walks into the apartment. Her mascara is smudged, like she's been crying.

I close my laptop and sit up. "What's wrong?" I ask, even though I have an awful, creeping feeling that I already know.

"Nothing," she says, and heads straight for the stairs.

I follow her up to her room. "Can I come in?"

"I guess," she says. It's not exactly a welcome, but at least she didn't tell me to go away.

I haven't been in her room much since we moved to this apartment. It looks like her old one, just smaller. The walls are almost completely covered with vintage magazine covers and photos of her and her friends. At our house, her walls were purple, but since this is a rental we have to leave the walls white. The rest of the room is artfully messy. Bits of fabric and sketchbooks filled with her fashion designs are everywhere. Her crafting desk is cluttered with sketches and spools of thread and drawing supplies. The sewing machine is half-covered by fabric. The only thing not covered with other things is her vanity. It's one of those old-school ones with a huge circular mirror surrounded by clear round bulbs.

"You don't seem like nothing's wrong," I say.

She sits down at her vanity and starts wiping foundation from her cheeks. "I'm fine," she says, voice bright. She tosses the wipe into the trash and gets out another one. "Ben and I broke up."

Wait.

"What happened?" I ask.

She shrugs. "I caught him kissing his ex."

This is really happening.

"Where?" I ask, picturing Ben in the shadow of lifeguard tower twenty-seven.

"At the beach. Behind one of the lifeguard stations," she says, with an eye roll and a scoff.

All at once, I feel the way I did earlier today. Light-headed and exhausted. Confused.

I sit on the edge of her bed.

"It's really not a big deal, Evie," she says.

"How can you say that?"

"Because it's not. There are a lot of other guys out there."

"But why even bother with guys at all?" I ask.

She stops wiping her face and turns to me. "Not everyone can be like you, Evie. I have actual human feelings."

"What does that mean?"

She turns back to the mirror. "The only thing you ever feel is angry at Dad."

I've wanted to tell her about Dad's affair so many times in the past year. If she knew, she'd be just as angry as I am. But Mom asked me not to. Sometimes I think telling her would be the kind thing to do. Isn't it always better to know the truth, to live without illusions?

I stand up and walk to the door.

Our eyes meet in the mirror. Her makeup is all gone now. Despite what she said about breaking up with Ben not being a big deal, she looks sad to me.

"I'm really sorry about Ben," I tell her, and slip out the door.

The truth is, I'm probably more upset by their breakup than Danica is. I don't understand what's happening to me.

It's one thing to hallucinate a vision of the future. It's something entirely different for that vision to come true.

CHAPTER 6

Not a Witch

WHEN I WAS younger, eight or maybe nine, I used to think Mom was a witch. Somehow she always knew things she shouldn't have. Like when I'd just picked my nose and eaten the booger. Or when I was reading under my blanket instead of sleeping.

I thought that one day, maybe when I turned ten, she'd sit me down and give me the talk:

"Evie," she'd say, "I am a witch from a long line of witches. Your grandma was a witch, and her mother before her, and her mother before that."

Then she'd put her hand on my face and say, "You too are a witch. A good witch." Then she'd tell me all about my powers and what an awesome responsibility they were.

We didn't have the witch talk on my tenth birthday. Instead, she and Dad talked to me about the sad, deep history of America and racism. They told me to pay attention to the world but also to live my life. To be joyous and fearless.

The witch talk didn't come on my eleventh or twelfth or thirteenth birthday either. By my fourteenth birthday, I didn't even think about witches or magic anymore.

But maybe I should've, because how else do I explain to myself what happened yesterday with Danica and Ben? Maybe Mom gave me witchy powers but forgot to tell me.

"What's with you today?" Martin asks me from across the table in the cafeteria. Martin is one of my best friends. He's white, with curly blond hair that grows faster than he can cut it. His favorite clothes are corduroy pants and cable-knit sweaters. This would be normal if he were a septuagenarian professor of English living in the cold English countryside. It's less normal for an eighteen-year-old boy living in Los Angeles, where the average temperature almost never calls for tweed.

We've been friends since second grade. We were in library class together on our very first day and wanted to check out the same book. The librarian said we had to share by reading it out loud to each other. One book led to another.

"I think I might be losing it," I say.

He rests his hand on his chin and considers me in his usual slow and careful way. "Tell me," he says.

"It's about Danica. She and Ben broke up."

He straightens. Martin's had a crush on Danica since the fourth grade, when he imprinted on her baby-goose style.

"When?" he asks.

"Last night."

He does a tiny, happy fist pump with himself. "What happened?"

"He cheated on her with his ex."

"Jesus, what an asshole," he says.

I wait for him to pull himself together. It takes a few seconds.

"So you're losing your mind because they broke up?" he asks.

"No. I mean, yes."

"I'm confused."

"I *knew* they were going to break up."

"Of course. They had to. We're destined to be," he says, smiling.

"Okay, but let's put destiny aside for a second," I say. "What I mean is I knew *when* they were going to break up. And *where*. And *why*." I take a very long breath. "I knew it all *before* they broke up."

He slow-blinks at me, which is what he does when he's contemplating something he doesn't understand. "Are you saying you can predict the future now?"

"Of course not." I take a sip of chocolate milk. "What I'm saying is I think maybe I can predict the future now."

Another slow blink from him. "This is where you say 'Once up on a time' and don't stop talking until you come to the end," he says.

I tell him exactly what happened yesterday. How I'd just ridden home from giving my books away to the old woman at the Little Free Library and how Ben and Danica—oblivious to the world—were kissing on the stoop. He winces at that detail, but there's nothing I can do about Danica's propensity to kiss people who are not Martin.

I tell him how the vision was like watching a movie. The first scene was Ben asking Danica out. Next was them kissing in front of me on the stoop. The third was them at the bonfire, and the fourth was Danica alone in her room.

I stop talking to gauge his reaction so far.

He's not looking at me as if he thinks I've finally lost my sanity, so I keep going. "But the craziest part is that when I got home, she told me they really did break up because she caught him kissing his ex on the beach."

"Was she really upset?" he asks quietly.

"She was fine," I say with a sigh. "But I need you to focus. I feel like you're maybe missing my very enormous point."

"Sorry, sorry," he says. "So you saw the whole history of their relationship from beginning to end? Past and present and future?"

"I don't understand why you're not telling me that I'm losing it." I lean forward and whisper, "I think I might be losing it."

"I'm not ruling it out, but I like to keep an open mind."

Martin's open-mindedness is actually one of my favorite things about him. I still remember the first time I needed to tell him to check his (white) privilege. He wasn't defensive. He just listened and learned.

If I told Cassidy (other best friend forever) about the vision, she would try to have me committed to a very expensive and upscale mental institution. Sophie (my other other best friend forever) would explain to me all the scientific reasons why what I'm saying is not possible. But for Martin, no idea is too outlandish to consider.

"Has it happened with anyone else?"

"No."

"So you're not seeing my romantic past and future right now?" he asks with an eyebrow waggle.

"Not possible, seeing as how you have neither," I say, grinning at him.

He smiles at me and flips me off at the same time.

"How about we do an experiment," he says after a while. "Maybe it only works on couples."

"What are you saying? I should stare at people?"

"How else are we going to figure out what's happening with you?"

"Fine," I say.

I scan the room. Shelley and Sheldon are sitting two tables over. Their coupledom is legendary. At first it was because of their ridiculously similar names. But now it's because of their longevity. They've been together for three years, since Shelley was a sophomore and Sheldon was a freshman. Every year, they get voted Couple Most Likely to Get Married.

I watch them for a good thirty seconds before looking back at Martin. "Nothing," I say.

He points to Dwight and Joel sitting by the windows. "How about them?"

I creepy-stare at them before turning back to Martin. "Nope," I say.

I try a few more times with other couples, but nothing happens. I look down at my mashed potatoes and carve little gravy rivulets with my fork. "I really am losing it," I say without looking up.

"My mom would say you have a lot going on. Your parents got divorced, and you found out your dad cheated, and you moved away from the house you grew up in, and it's second semester senior year. She'd say stress is a killer."

Martin's mom is a psychiatrist. She'd definitely say all that before launching into her speech about how weekly therapy sessions should be required for everyone, but most especially for middle and high school students.

"And your mom still won't talk about anything?" he asks.

"She doesn't think there's anything to talk about. Danica too. I'm the only one who's still stuck," I say. I don't expect to cry, but tears are suddenly burning behind my eyes.

Martin hands me a napkin before I can even look for one. I dab my eyes quickly, not wanting anyone to see.

My eyes drift back to Shelley and Sheldon. They're sitting side by side now, still making moony faces at each other. Shelley leans into Sheldon, pressing her shoulder into his. He throws his arm around her and they kiss.

And I see.

CHAPTER 7

Shelley and Sheldon

A SUNNY MORNING in Mr. Armstrong's US History classroom. He's stalking the aisle, looking for cheaters. As soon as his back is turned, Sheldon hands Shelley a note. Shelley opens it and giggles. The note reads:

> Would you like to go out with me?
> ❏ YES!
> ❏ YES!!
> ❏ YES!!!
> ❏ All of the above!

She takes out her pen and checks all the boxes, including *All of the above!*

Nighttime on a Ferris wheel high above Santa Monica pier. Shelley stares at Sheldon but looks away when she's caught. Sheldon stares at Shelley but looks away when he's caught. They do this for a while. The Ferris wheel seat is wide enough that their bodies aren't touching, but you can tell they want to.

Finally, Shelley runs her hands over her bare arms and shivers a fake shiver.

Sheldon slides closer and wraps his arm around her shoulders. The ride attendant sees them making out and doesn't kick them off until after they've been around six or seven times.

This moment right now: Shelley and Sheldon sharing a quick kiss in the cafeteria.

Shelley reading her college acceptance letter on her laptop. Sheldon is reading it over her shoulder. They're both happy for her. But sad too.

Sheldon helping Shelley pack for college. He finds his "Would you like to go out with me?" note in her desk drawer. He slips it into her suitcase for her to find later.

Sheldon reading an email from Shelley. The subject line is "I'm sorry."

Sheldon sitting alone on the Ferris wheel high above Santa Monica pier with no one beside him who needs warming up.

CHAPTER 8

Zoltar

THE VISION STOPS and I'm back in the cafeteria. Martin is staring at me with wide, urgent eyes. "It just happened again, didn't it?" he asks.

I nod, and nod again. "They're going to break up."

He looks over at them and then back at me. "No way. Those guys are forever."

"No," I say. "They're not."

I tell him exactly what I saw: the note where he asks her out, their first date on the Ferris wheel, her getting her college acceptance letter, him helping her to pack for college and finally him alone on the Ferris wheel.

"I think it's the kiss," I whisper. "The only difference between the first time I stared at them and the second time is that they were kissing."

Martin's nodding like he's already figured that out. "Okay, okay," he says, "we need to try to understand what we're dealing with."

I'm glad he's thinking logically, because I'm not. All I know is that what's happening to me is not possible. Except it is possible, because it's happening to me.

"We need to know if what you're seeing is real."

"We already know," I say. "Danica and Ben, remember?"

"But she's your sister, and you know him a little, right? You don't know Shelley and Sheldon at all."

"So what do you want me to do? Go over there and ask Shelley if she's going to break Sheldon's heart after she goes away to college next year?"

He snaps his fingers. "I have an idea," he says as he slides out of his seat. "All couples love telling their origin stories." He goes over to them and sits.

After a few seconds, Shelley lights up and then Sheldon does too.

It's only five minutes before he comes back over to me. "Everything you said about their first meeting was right," he says, amazed and disbelieving at the same time. "Tell me again *exactly* what happened yesterday. Don't leave anything out."

I tell him again.

He asks a lot of questions about the old woman and the Little Free Library:

> "You didn't see her at first and then suddenly she was just there?" and

> "You found a book about . . . *ballroom dancing*?" and

> "When you looked back she was just gone?"

Strung together like that, his questions make me feel like I should've known something was up. But why would I think something was up?

He stares out across the cafeteria, thinking. After a while he laughs and shakes his head. "I think you got Zoltared," he says.

"What are you talking about?"

"Did you ever see the movie *Big* with Tom Hanks?" he asks.

"Was this movie made in the last twenty years?"

"It's a classic," he says. Martin is unapologetic about his ancient tastes. Along with old movies, he loves old songs, old books and clothing best left for old men. Today, for example, he's wearing a ten-thousand-year-old tweed blazer with elbow patches.

"Just listen," he says, "*Big* is about this twelve-year-old kid. He's at an amusement park trying to impress a girl by getting on one of the big-kid rides. The problem is he's too short for it and they won't let him on. He gets upset and takes off. Eventually he finds one of those old fortune-teller machines."

"Lemme guess, the fortune-teller is named Zoltar?"

"Look who's so smart," he says. "Anyway, the kid puts a coin in and makes a wish to be big. Zoltar does his thing and a ticket comes out saying the kid's wish will be granted. The kid's about to take off when he realizes the machine was unplugged the whole time, so how could it spit out a ticket?"

"Then what happens?" I ask.

"The next morning when he wakes up he's all grown up."

We both sit there quietly for a minute. I connect the east and west tributaries in my mashed potatoes. After a while, the four-minute-warning bell rings. We head for the door.

"Martin," I say, "magic isn't real."

"I know," he says.

"Do you?"

"Yes."

"I feel like you don't," I say.

I take one last look back at Shelley and Sheldon. Instead of a happy couple, all I see is Sheldon alone on the Ferris wheel, high over Santa Monica.

"Do you still have the ballroom dancing book?" he asks.

I realize that I never actually took it out of my backpack. I pull it out and flip through the pages, running my fingers over the diagrams. Am I supposed to teach myself how to dance?

Martin takes the book from me and thumbs through the pages himself. He stops and turns to me. "I think I figured it out," he says slowly. "But you have to keep an open mind."

"My mind could not be more open," I say.

He holds the book so I can see what he sees. There's an *If lost, please return to* stamp on the last page. Underneath, there's an address for a place called La Brea Dance.

"This is it," he says, sounding very excited and very certain. "This is what you're supposed to do next."

CHAPTER 9

So Fatal a Contagion

ACCORDING TO THEIR website, La Brea Dance is a small dance studio specializing in group and private ballroom dance lessons "For Weddings! Parties! Or Just for the Love of Dance!" It's owned by an older Black couple—Archibald and Maggie Johnson. On the site there's a small black-and-white photo of them smiling into each other's eyes.

It turns out I've ridden by it hundreds of times without noticing it was there. It's only ten minutes from my apartment, on the route I take to school every morning.

I hop off my bike and look around for a rack to lock it to, but (naturally) there isn't one. I'll have to take it inside with me. It looks like the actual studio is at the top of a long, steep and narrow staircase. I pick up my bike and begin the hike.

Almost every inch of the stairway walls is covered with dance memorabilia. It feels a little like I'm ascending to ballroom dance heaven. There's a poster for a movie called *Swing Time* with Fred Astaire and Ginger Rogers. There's the *Mad Hot Ballroom* poster with two larger-than-life brown kids dancing in front of the New York City skyline. There are dance trophies and medals and framed records. Close to the top of the staircase, there's a life-sized poster of a man and woman of indeterminate age wrapped tightly around each other. The woman is wearing a scarlet dress with matching heels. The man is wearing a blinding white tux. I think the pained look on their faces is supposed to be passion, but it looks like actual physical agony. I'd guess the pain is from the (Photoshopped) flames they're dancing in. Across the top of the poster it says *Come Feel the Heat.* Across the bottom, written into the flames, it says *Argentine Tango.*

When I finally get to the top of the staircase, I lean my bike against the wall and stretch my aching arms. There's a small office with a receptionist's window just ahead, but no one's in it. On the sill, I see pamphlets for lots of dances—salsa, bachata, waltz, etc. I take one of each and flip through them while waiting for the receptionist to come back. Occasionally a door down the hall opens and salsa music drifts out toward me. I wait ten minutes before deciding to ring the tiny bell on the sill.

A woman—white and tiny, with severely cut jet-black bangs—stomps down the hallway toward me. She's wearing an astonishingly red asymmetrical dress with long fringe (also astonishingly red) across the bottom and perfectly matching bright-red strappy stilettos. Her fringe sways madly with each stomp. She's an exploding firecracker in human form.

Once she's in the office, she grabs the bell from the window-sill and tosses it into a drawer. Satisfied, she peers through the window at me and then improbably—given the situation with the stomping and the bell—smiles. "You are interested in the waltz, I see."

Except for when she says it, it sounds like *You are eeenterested in zee waltz, I zee.* Her accent is vaguely Eastern European and very heavy.

"What? No," I say, putting the pamphlets down. I open my backpack and take out the *Instructions for Dancing* book. "I just came to return this," I say. "It says to return it to this address."

She takes it from me and flips through it for exactly two seconds before tossing it to the side. "Come, Saturday morning is perfect time for you to come in. Best waltzing class in history of world is about to begin."

She takes off down the hallway.

"Wait," I say. "I can't just leave my bike here."

She opens a door with a sign that reads *Studio 5* and tells me it'll be okay in there.

Once I'm done stashing my bike, we walk down the hall to another studio. She holds the door open for me. When I hesitate, she stomps one foot. "You want to learn or no?"

In my head, I hear Martin imploring me to keep an open mind. I remind myself that the reason I'm here is to figure out what's happening to me and that this is the only clue I have.

"Yes, I want to learn," I say, and go inside.

The studio is a wide-open space with hardwood floors, barres for stretching and floor-to-ceiling mirrors. Twenty or so people are standing in pairs next to the windows in the back of the room.

"These are clients," says the woman. "Most of them have wedding coming up and need waltz for first dance."

Almost all of the couples are in their late twenties and early thirties. I spy a few engagement rings. Some of them seem eager and others seem nervous. I hope I don't see any of them kissing.

The woman turns to me. "But where is special friend? Cannot ballroom dance alone."

"I don't have a special friend," I say.

"Why not?"

Is she really asking me about my love life right now? Mercifully, the older Black couple I saw on the website last night walks into the room. Exploding firecracker woman shifts her attention to them, and I'm saved from having to explain why I don't have a special friend.

"Welcome to La Brea Dance," says the older woman, Maggie.

In my entire life, I don't think I've ever seen anyone so regal. She looks like she's just assumed the throne of a small but powerful Caribbean island nation. She has thick gray dreads that are piled high on her head, with a few strands framing her bright brown face. Her ball gown is high-necked and pale blue and made from sequined lace, tulle and (I'm pretty sure) the diaphanous wings of actual fairies.

Her husband, Archibald, is tall and thin, with a bald head and a salt-and-pepper mustache. He's wearing a white tux with white suspenders and a bow tie that matches Maggie's dress perfectly. He's so dapper, I'm pretty sure he's the reason the word *dapper* was invented.

He claps his hands together. "Today you'll be learning both

the regular English waltz, which is slow and boring, and the faster Viennese waltz, which is much more interesting."

"Don't be nervous," Maggie says. "Nobody ever died waltzing."

"Although there was a time they were persecuted for it," Archibald adds.

He goes on to give us a small history lesson. He tells us that the waltz is the oldest of the ballroom dances, that it began as a peasant dance in Vienna in the seventeenth century and that the name is from the old German word *walzen,* which means "to turn or glide."

Then he tucks his hands into his pockets and rocks back on his heels. I can tell the next part is his favorite from the way his eyes twinkle madly. "Everyone hated the waltz when it was first introduced to high society. Religious leaders thought it was vulgar and sinful," he says, and points at Maggie's dress. "Because the women wore ball gowns when they danced, they had to hold one corner off the ground so they wouldn't trip. Can anyone guess why this was a problem?" he asks.

No one can, so he answers his own question. "The problem is ankles," he says. "Sexy, sexy ankles."

Maggie picks up a corner of her gown and wiggles her foot. Everyone laughs.

He tells us that when the waltz arrived in England, one English newspaper thought it was so "obscene" that it printed an editorial warning parents against exposing their daughters to "so fatal a contagion."

He smiles. "Isn't it funny how time changes everything?" he asks.

Maggie walks over to the record player and moves the needle to the record. Archibald dims the lights. "Fallin'" by Alicia Keys starts playing and they begin to dance.

I've seen ballroom dance shows on TV before, but that doesn't compare to the romance and drama of seeing it in real life. It's not like they're telling a story with their bodies, more like they're dancing an emotion. When they get to the Viennese waltz, it's like they're skipping through air. They dance by me, and Maggie's ball gown makes a small tornado at my feet.

I'm enchanted. Everyone is. Some of the couples move closer to each other, caught up in the magic of them. As the song ends, he spins her one last time and bends her into a dip. The room sighs into quiet for a few seconds and then explodes with applause.

I'm clapping too, but mostly I'm watching them. I don't think they've noticed the applause. I don't think they've noticed anything but each other. They're still holding the dip, his hand on her back, her arm on his shoulder. They're breathing hard and gazing at each other with so much love, it's almost too bright to look at. A few more seconds pass before they turn into a bow. We all cheer so loud, you'd think someone sank a game-winning three-pointer instead of just ending a waltz.

Firecracker woman ushers me out of the studio as soon as the actual lesson begins.

She turns to me once we're back in the hallway. "What is word you Americans are always using? *Amazing*. They are amazing, no?"

"I've never seen anything like it," I say, and I don't just mean their dancing.

Once we're back at the reception office, she sits in front of the computer.

"What is name?" she asks, wiggling her fingers over the keyboard.

"Evie," I say, before rushing to add that I'm not ready to sign up for lessons yet.

"But if not now, then when?" she asks. "You could do it even without special friend."

"I just need some time to think about it," I say, backing away.

She sighs and stares at the screen, disappointed. "Well, it was nice to meet you anyway." She leaves the office and heads back down the hallway.

I walk toward the studio where I left my bike and hear the distinct trill of the bell coming from inside. I slow down. The lights are not on. Which means someone who is not me is riding my bike around a dark dance studio.

The door is just slightly open. I move closer to it.

"I'm sorry, Jess. No, don't cry. Please don't cry," pleads a guy's voice.

Holy crap. I'm pretty sure I'm overhearing a breakup. I wait, expecting to hear a sniffled response, until I realize the guy must be talking to someone on the phone.

"I didn't mean to break— Yeah, no, you're right, I'm a jerk. . . . I'm sorry, Jess. . . . No, I didn't know you bought . . . Wait, when did you buy a dress? . . . Yesterday?"

Overhearing this conversation reminds me of the visions. Why am I being subjected to knowing the secret lives of other people?

43

There are lot of things I'd rather do than have to turn on the lights and interrupt this emotional cataclysm. But I also need my bike so I can go home and forget about this disappointing trip.

"But, Jess, we broke up like ten months ago," says the voice. "I don't even go to school there anymore. Why would you buy a prom dress? Okay, okay . . . yeah, I'll talk to you later. Okay, don't cry. Okay. I'm sorry."

My bike bell trills again and the studio lights flicker on. I take it as my signal that the conversation is over, and push open the door. Just like the other studio, this one has floor-to-ceiling mirrors, so instead of seeing just one guy riding my bike slowly around the room, I see many of them.

The first thing I notice is his face—all brown skin, dark eyes and cheekbones. The second thing I notice is that he's very tall. Gratuitously tall, really. He looks ridiculous on my short bike. The third thing is his hair—long, skinny dreads dipped in blue and piled high on top of his head. So maybe not quite as tall as I thought, since his hair is responsible for at least three inches. The fourth thing is his hands, which are giant and completely dwarf my handlebars. The fifth thing I notice is I'm noticing a lot of things about him. So I stop.

"Umm," I say.

He swings one absurdly long leg over the bike and hops off.

He tilts the bike toward me. "I'm guessing this is yours," he says.

I step into the studio. "Did you adjust my seat?"

"Yeah, sorry about that," he says. "Long legs." He lifts one leg and wiggles it. To demonstrate how tall he is.

I notice him some more.

He's wearing ripped jeans, black canvas shoes and a teal-blue T-shirt with a line drawing of a unicorn. It says *Not the Only One* in cursive. Could he be any more hipster? Dyed dreads, torn jeans, old-school shoes and ironic T-shirt. Any three of those things would've been enough. Four is too much. He's a hipster overachiever.

"Nice bike, by the way," he says when I take the handlebars. "Never seen one of those. What kind is it?"

"Beach cruiser," I say, wondering how he's never seen one. These things are all over every beach in Southern California. It's true, though, that mine's really nice. Tasseled handlebars, wide wicker basket, fenders and a step-through frame so I can ride it with a skirt on and not show my goods to the world. Dad got it for me for my birthday before everything fell apart.

I flip down the kickstand so I can adjust the seat from tall-hipster-guy height to not-tall-non-hipster-girl height.

"I was gonna change it back right after I got done—"

"Breaking Jess's heart," I say, finishing his sentence for him with the thing he was probably not going to say.

He looks away from me, embarrassed, and then palms the entire back of his neck with a single enormous hand. There's a tattoo on the back of his biceps. It's either an X or a plus sign. Hipster-trait tally at five.

"My name's X, by the way," he says.

I look up. "Ex? Like an *e* followed by an *x*?"

"Short for Xavier. Everyone calls me X."

"So that's an X tattooed on your arm? Aren't you supposed to tattoo someone else's name?"

45

He lifts his arm and frowns at his own biceps. "That's not me. I'm in a band. X Machine."

"Oh. So the band is named after you?" I don't know why I'm giving him such a hard time. Maybe for the sake of this Jess girl.

He frowns some more and looks a little lost. "It's just a cool name," he says.

I finish adjusting my seat and flip up the kickstand. "Well, nice meeting—"

"What's your name?" he asks.

"Yvette," I say. I don't know why I don't say Evie.

"Thanks for letting me borrow your bike, Yvette," he says, and gives me a grin so spectacular it makes me (temporarily) stupid.

Technically, it's not a perfect smile. He has a small gap between his front teeth, and the right side of his face scrunches a little too much. Still, I have no doubt it's a grin that works wonders for him. It gets him A grades on B papers, into sold-out concerts and the phone numbers of heads of state. When the time comes, it'll get him into heaven, even though he should clearly be headed in the other direction.

It's a grin that works well for him. I know because it's working well on me.

I force my brain cells to stop abdicating their duties and remind myself that he's not my type.

Mainly because I don't have a type. Not anymore.

And even back when I did have a type, it was never anyone so . . . obvious. Tall, hipster-hot and in a band? I mean, he's the definition of a heartbreaker, right? Literally, he was just break-

46

ing someone's heart. It doesn't matter that he seemed genuinely pained while he was doing it.

"Okay," I say. "I'm leaving now."

He raises a single eyebrow and I almost laugh. For a second, I feel like I'm a character in one of my old romance books. Raising a single eyebrow is such a Classic Romance Guy Characteristic.

I grab my bike and head out and tell myself I'm not in a romance novel.

CHAPTER 10

Classic Romance Guy Characteristics: A Nonexhaustive List

- Aforementioned uncanny ability to raise a single eyebrow.
- Propensity to smirk. Or to smile lopsided, self-deprecating smiles.
- Inability to choose appropriately sized clothing. T-shirts are often too tight and stretch distractingly across (well-muscled) chests and toned biceps.
- Unusual eyes. Typically one color flecked with another color. E.g.: "His eyes are green flecked with gold."

CHAPTER 11

The Formula for Heartbreak

IT TURNS OUT that people kiss all the time.

All. The. Time.

It happens again later that same day. I'm in the baking aisle at the grocery, picking up the (real, Tahitian) vanilla beans Mom wants. There's a man musing on the difference between baking powder and baking soda. A woman—his girlfriend—tells him it's cute how much he doesn't know. She leans in and kisses him. The entire history of their relationship plays out in front of me, just like it did with Danica and Ben, and Shelley and Sheldon.

They met through a dating app and had their first date at a coffee shop. The first time he said I love you was over text, with red heart emojis. She called him right away and told him she loved him too. They went ring shopping together. He proposed to her at the same coffee shop where they had their first date.

Sometime soon, he's going to get a job offer for someplace in South America. He's going to tell her he wants to break up and take the job and go on an adventure. She's going to tell him that's what marriage is. He's going to tell her that marriage may be an adventure, but it's not one he wants to take, not yet and not with her.

The rest of the week goes by in the same way. I have at least one vision every day. I'm amazed at all the different ways people connect.

There's the girl who watches the same movie three times in a row so she can keep flirting with the usher between showings.

And the boy who pretends not to know the rules of football so the other boy will explain it to him.

I figure out some of the rules for the visions. They only appear the first time I see a couple kiss. I know because I accidentally caught another Shelley/Sheldon kiss and nothing happened. I also think the couple might need to be in love. I've seen two first-date kisses and didn't have a vision for either one. The number of scenes in each vision varies by couple. I think I'm only seeing the most important moments in their love story. I don't know what or who decides which moments are most important.

I spend a lot of time searching the internet. One of the great and also terrible things about the internet is you can always find a community of people interested in the same things you are. Great because some interests are pretty wonderful. Romance novel reading, for example. Terrible because some interests are awful. I'm not going to give any examples. No matter how long I search, I don't find any support groups for people who are suddenly able to see other people's romantic futures.

Another week passes, and the visions accumulate and wash over me. I'm not sure how to feel. Mostly I feel every emotion. Shock that this impossible thing is happening to me. Guilt at invading people's privacy. Fascination at seeing their private lives. Sadness at seeing their relationships end.

And that's the thing all the relationships have in common. They all end.

The girl who saw the movie three times? She got bored with her boyfriend after a few weeks and started going to a different theater.

The boy who pretended not to understand football? His homophobic family moved him away to prevent him from being with the boy he loved.

What I've learned over the last three weeks is that all my old romance novels ended too quickly. Chapters were missing from the end. If they told the real story—the entire story—each couple would've eventually broken up, due to neglect or boredom or betrayal or distance or death.

Given enough time, all love stories turn into heartbreak stories.

Heartbreak = love + time.

CHAPTER 12

Lesson Learning

"I'M THINKING ABOUT getting breast implants," Cassidy says, apropos of nothing. "What do you guys think?"

It's the first Sunday of spring break, and Cassidy, Martin, Sophie, and I are where we usually are on Sunday mornings: Surf City Waffle. The story is that when it came time to name this place, the owner's six-year-old drew a picture of a giant waffle surfing on a sea of blueberry syrup. The facts that we're not in Surf City (officially Huntington Beach or Santa Cruz, depending on who you ask) and are ten miles away from the beach and that waffles don't surf matters not at all. The waffles are delicious.

"But why?" I ask her, even though I know she has no intention of getting implants. Cassidy is prone to sudden, fleeting obsessions. Like the time she was going to get an enormous Valkyrie tattooed across her back, or the time she wanted to become a professional trapeze artist.

She shrugs like it's not a big deal. "I just think they could be bigger." She tucks in her chin and peers down at her breasts. "Do you think everyone will be able to tell?"

"Don't do it," Sophie says. "They're great the way they are." I'm pretty sure she blushes as she says it.

"I'll definitely be able to tell," Martin says as if he's a breast expert.

"Oh, please," Cassidy says, laughing. "You wouldn't know a real breast if it hit you in the face."

He scowls, but not in a serious way. Unless he's been keeping secrets from us all, Martin's never seen or touched a pair of breasts in his eighteen years on the planet. "One day my ship will come in," he says.

"Will your ship be shaped like breasts?" I ask.

"I don't think breasts are seaworthy," says Sophie.

"Well, they definitely float," Cassidy says, doing a weird bobbing thing with her own breasts that only Cassidy would do.

Sophie laughs at Cassidy's antics, covering her mouth with her hands the way she always does when she thinks she's laughing too hard.

Cassidy waits for her to stop laughing and then immediately does the bobbing move again.

Sophie laughs even harder this time. Finally, she takes her hands from her face. "Stop making me laugh," she says, breathless.

"Not my fault you think I'm so funny," Cassidy says.

"But you *are* so funny," Sophie says. The way she says it is almost shy.

I look back and forth between them. If I didn't know better, I'd think they were flirting.

Martin, Sophie, Cassidy and I don't have an epic origin

story. From the outside looking in, I guess we seem kind of unlikely, if you judge friendships on race alone. Cassidy is white, with incredibly wealthy and neglectful producer parents. Sophie is mixed, Black French mom and Korean American dad, both scientists. Martin I've already described. His dad died when he was a baby.

The four of us have been friends since sixth grade, when a scheduling fluke put us—and only us—into the same study period. We started out in the four corners of the room but eventually met in the middle, killing time by trading jokes and gossip. We've been friends ever since.

"Let's talk about the route," Martin says, trying to bring us all back to the task at hand, which is planning our epic post-graduation cross-country road trip.

He pushes our plates aside and spreads out a laminated map of the United States.

"You really are from the Stone Age," I say, teasing him for having an actual paper map.

He ignores my teasing. "I think we should stick to a northerly route," he says.

I nod. The boy withers in temperatures above eighty degrees. Sophie says something about wanting to see some kind of biosphere in Arizona. Cassidy wants to see the kitschy stuff, giant balls of twine and all that. Martin only cares about the houses of famous dead authors like Emily Dickinson and Edgar Allan Poe. I have a list of places I want to visit too: Bryce Canyon National Park, which looks like another planet in photos, and a couple of the dark-sky parks in Utah and Ohio. I have this vision of open skies and stars and freedom.

I stare out the window as they plan. Ordinarily, I'd be paying attention. I've wanted to take this trip since freshman year. It's hard to believe it's only a few months away now.

But I'm not paying attention. All I can think about is the visions and how my trip to La Brea Dance a week ago was a total dead end.

"You're not listening even a little bit, are you?" Martin says, nudging me with his shoulder.

I look up and give him a small smile. "Sorry," I say.

"What's wrong?" asks Sophie.

Before I can answer, Cassidy interrupts. "Since when does your sister wear tennis skirts?" she asks, staring toward the door.

"Since never," I say, turning to look. Sure enough, Danica's here, outfitted in full tennis gear. White bandana, white T-shirt, white pleated skirt, white tennis shoes. She would look ridiculous if she didn't look so fabulous. Her new boyfriend, whose name I can't remember for the life of me—it's something active, to do with sports or hunting—is dressed exactly the same way, except for shorts instead of a skirt.

Martin sinks low into the booth. He stabs my leftover waffle with his fork and moves it to his own plate.

"Who is that guy, anyway?" he asks.

"Archer," says Sophie. Sophie always knows everyone's name.

I'm suddenly frustrated with Martin. When's he going to give up on Danica? It's not like love is worth all the pain.

"Can we just go back to planning?" I ask, louder than I mean to.

Sophie and Cassidy exchange a look.

Martin slumps down farther into the booth.

"What's going on with you, Eves?" Sophie asks.

"Sorry," I say. "I didn't mean to—"

"Just tell us what's wrong," says Cassidy.

I don't know where to start. I definitely don't want to have to explain the visions to Sophie and Cassidy. First I'd have to prove to them that they're real, and then I'd have to explain why I haven't told them since the beginning.

"Really, I'm okay," I say, and give them a big smile. "Sorry I'm being such a downer."

I look down at the map and give it (and our plans) my full attention.

After about an hour of planning, Sophie and Cassidy take off. Cassidy has to go to a "sucky fundraiser in Beverly Hills" with her parents, and Sophie is judging a second-grade science fair at the California Science Center.

"Sorry I snapped at you," I say to Martin once they're gone. I tell him that going to La Brea Dance didn't help. "I don't know what else to do. How do I get the visions to stop?"

He pours both strawberry and blueberry syrup onto his waffle before answering. "Remember that movie I told you about, *Big*? He doesn't get to change back into a little kid until he's learned his lesson," he says. "All those movies are like that. You're supposed to learn something."

"Okay, but those movies are *fiction*. This is my *real* life."

"I know," he says. He's quiet for a while and then says: "I think you should go back to the dance studio."

"But why?"

"There's a reason their address was in that book. Try again. Go with the flow. You don't have anything to lose."

I make a sound between a sigh and a groan. He's right, of course. I have to go back. I don't really have any other options.

"Maybe you're supposed to learn to dance," he says once we're outside on the sidewalk.

I unlock my bike. "That makes no sense at all," I say.

"I know, but I'm sure I'm right about this," he says. And then, because he's actually an old man, he bursts into "Dancing Queen" by Abba. *"You are the dancing queen. Young and sweet. Only seventeen."*

He laugh-sings three more verses before I finally, finally get him to be quiet.

CHAPTER 13

Dancing with the Flow

"OH, IT'S YOU, girl without dance partner," firecracker woman says when I get to La Brea Dance after school the next day. "Nice to see you."

"Hi, it's nice to see you too," I say. "I'm Evie," I add, even though I told her the last time I was here. I'm hoping she'll use my actual name and not forever refer to me as "girl without dance partner."

She nods, and there's a tiny smile at the corner of her mouth that makes me think she knows exactly how outrageous she is.

"Did not think I would see you again," she says.

I don't confess that I didn't think I'd see her again either. "I was hoping to sign up for a trial lesson."

"Wonderful. Which one?" she asks, looking down at her computer. "I pull up schedule."

"What's the easiest one you have? I've never done this before."

She looks up and peers through the window at me. "Oh, you are nervous, I can hear."

"Maybe a little bit," I admit.

She springs up from her chair. "No, no, not to worry. Not

everybody can dance good, but everybody can dance." She leans closer to the sill. "You have time now?"

I start to say no and that I only dropped by to sign up, not to actually get started, but I stop myself. Yesterday Martin told me I needed to go with the flow.

"Sure, I have time," I say.

She enters my info in the computer and then takes the bell out of her desk drawer and puts it on the sill. "I hate you," she says to it.

I laugh and she does too. She leaves the office and waves for me to follow her. "Lucky for you, my Intro to Bachata class starts now. Not to worry. Is easy dance, and this is beginner class."

She takes off down the hallway. Her outfit today is a deeply purple, mid-thigh-length asymmetrical dress with gold shoes that are at least three inches high. I don't know how she walks in them, much less dances.

When we get to the studio, I'm disappointed to see only a few people. I was hoping I'd be able to hide away in the back.

She claps to get everyone's attention. "Hello, everyone. I am Fifi and I am instructor."

She pauses, arms akimbo, expecting us to respond to her greeting. "Hi, Fifi," we say, as if we're all in some sort of dance recovery program.

"Today, I will introduce you to bachata. At beginning you will not be good. Some of you will be like clumsy newborn baby octopus, but by the end you will be better. You will see, I am fabulous instructor."

She makes us form a single line in front of the mirrors.

"Now I teach you basics. First I show steps for leader, and then I show for follower." She places her left hand against her stomach, raises her right hand into the air and snaps her fingers to keep time. "Is simple," she says, swaying her hips while taking two small steps to the right. "One, two, three, pop." On the pop, she juts her left hip out dramatically and then repeats the movement going to the left. "One, two, three, pop."

Her movements are precise but somehow still fluid and sexy. She repeats the step two more times before telling us it's our turn. Since there's no music, the only sounds are her voice and the shuffle and tap of our feet against hardwood. There's something relaxing and even a little comforting about the way we're all moving and breathing together.

After a while she moves us on from side basic to forward basic, which is the same step, only forward and backward. Like she promised, the steps aren't hard, and she's satisfied that we know what we're doing pretty quickly.

"Okay, now you know basic step, but real dance is in the hips. Watch me." This time when she does the basic side step, her hips do a figure-eight pattern that completely changes the feel of the dance. It's sexier, more dramatic. "Some people call this Cuban motion. You see it in dances like merengue and salsa. I call it infinity hips." She demonstrates a few more times before it's our turn again.

Infinity hips, it turns out, is very hard to do. It's not long before we're all laughing and giggling at how very finite our own hips are. I see very few figure eights, more like deformed circles or wobbly lines.

She sighs a dramatic sigh and tells us to stop. "Not to worry.

Always starts like this." She tells the couples to partner up and then beckons me over. "Now I demonstrate how to hold each other." She adjusts me into "open position" and leads us all through the basic steps again.

The lesson is so much fun, I barely notice the hour go by. I forget about the visions. Instead, I concentrate on listening to the music and moving my body to it. Fifi is funny and encouraging and firm. She knows exactly how to break the steps down in a way that makes sense to each person.

For the last dance, she chooses a song with a faster tempo, dims the lights and tells us to pretend we're in a club. She partners with me and we all dance together. It's hilarious and messy, but—like she said we would—we've come a long way since the beginning of class.

The song ends. Everyone's breathing hard but smiling, obviously happy and energized.

Fifi turns the lights back up. "Okay, I see you next week. Make sure to practice so not forget. I do not want to teach basic step again."

I hang back as people filter out, even though I'm not sure what I'm waiting for. A sign of what to do next, I guess.

"I can see you enjoyed very much, yes?" she asks when it's just the two of us.

"You're a great instructor," I tell her, still breathless.

"Yes, I know," she says with a smile. "You are good student, very natural. Still need to work on hips, but you have good head for steps and excellent timing in body."

I smile even wider. I'm surprised by how much I like her compliment. I had way more fun than I expected to. I can also feel that ballroom might be one of those things where it's easy enough to learn the basics but much harder to get all the subtleties of movement.

She looks me up and down, contemplating something. "I have proposition for you," she says. "There is competition they have every year. LA Danceball, is called."

She tells me all about it. LA Danceball is one of the largest ballroom dance competitions for professional and amateur dancers in Southern California. They have lots of different age group and proficiency categories. Her proposition is that I enter the Amateur Under 21 category on behalf of the studio.

"Are you kidding?" I ask. "That was the first ballroom dance lesson I've ever taken."

She waves me off. "Is amateur category. And like I say, you have potential."

I shake my head. "Why do you even want me to enter?"

"If you win, studio gets free advertising, and maybe we get some more clients." A worried frown flashes across her face. I get the feeling the studio not only wants more clients, it *needs* them.

"I don't know," I say.

"Come, come. There is reason you walk in here in first place, no?"

She's right, of course. There *is* a reason I walked in here in the first place. Is this what I'm supposed to do? Enter a ballroom dance competition? Martin is in my head again, insisting that I go with the flow.

"But, Fifi, I don't even have a partner," I say.

"Not to worry," she says. "I have perfect someone."

CHAPTER 14

Dance Number One

THE PERFECT SOMEONE isn't there when I show up at the studio after school the next day, but the owners—Archibald and Maggie—are.

"You must be Evie," Maggie says as soon as I walk in.

"That's me," I say, giving them a small wave.

I forgot how striking they are. He's wearing a gray tux. She's wearing a glittering fuchsia gown and bright makeup. Unlike last time, her locs aren't pinned up. They cascade around her shoulders.

"Fifi didn't bully you into doing this, did she, dear?" Archibald asks.

"I am not bully," Fifi protests.

"Did she guilt you?" Maggie asks.

"No bullying or guilting," I say. Maybe my suspicion from yesterday is right. The studio does need money. "I just thought this would be fun." And it's true that I think it could be fun, but that's not why I'm doing it.

"Well, that's wonderful, dear," says Maggie. "I want you to know there is no pressure for you to win."

"There is itsy-bitsy little bit of pressure," Fifi interjects.

There eez eeetsy-beetsy leetle beet of pressure.

"Fiona Karapova, don't you dare—"

But before Maggie can start scolding Fifi, the studio door opens behind me.

"Ahh, here is partner now," Fifi says.

I turn around. It's the boy I met in studio five the first time I was here. Xavier. X.

"It's you," I say.

"It's me," he agrees.

"But why?" I ask.

"You mean that existentially or what?" He smirks and raises an eyebrow at me, displaying not one but two Classic Romance Guy Characteristics.

Maggie interrupts our staring contest. "You know each other?"

"No," I say.

"Yes," he says. "Yvette, right?"

"He stole my bike," I explain, stomping out the infinitesimal and completely uncalled-for spark of happiness I feel that he remembered my name.

"Borrowed it," he clarifies.

"So he could break up with his girlfriend," I explain some more.

"We were already broken up," he clarifies some more.

"She bought a prom dress," I remind him.

In my periphery, I see Archibald and Maggie watching us with mouths slightly open.

I know how this looks. It looks like we're bantering, like

sparks are flying between us like in witty, old romantic comedies. It looks like the start of something. But I promise you, there are no sparks. Nothing here is on fire.

Archibald chuckles. "Well, Evie, this is our grandson, Xavier."

"It's just X, Gramps," X says. He gives Maggie a hug.

"Come," Fifi says to X. "Stand next to girl so I can see you together."

By "girl" she means me.

X walks his long legs over to me.

"We will have to do something about clothes," Fifi says as she scrutinizes us both. "But they are good match height-wise," she says to Archibald and Maggie. "And both very good-looking. Especially X," she says, and waggles her eyebrows like some sort of demented cartoon character.

"Fiona, be a dear and don't undress my grandchild with your eyes," says Maggie.

"You prefer I should use my hands?" asks Fifi.

Archibald guffaws an actual guffaw.

X cough-laughs into his fist.

To be fair, Maggie kind of walked into that one.

After we're done laughing, both Archibald and Maggie explain how the competition works. We'll be competing for the Top Studio Amateur prize in the Nightclub Dance category. Nightclub is made up of five dances: bachata, salsa, West Coast swing, hustle and Argentine tango. Westside Dance Studio, their main competitor, wins the prize every year.

"But not this year," Maggie says with a determined nod.

They—Archibald and Maggie—touch each other the entire

time they're explaining. A small hand squeeze here, a quick caress to the face there. You can practically see love bubbles floating out of their eyes when they look at each other.

After they're done, they wish us luck and leave the studio, arms around each other's waists, laughing about something.

Fifi waits for the door to close before turning to X. "Forty-three years your grandparents have been married, yes?"

"Sounds about right," he says.

"You live with them. Tell me something: they are so lovey-dovey at home too?"

X nods and laughs. "Never seen anything like it either. They're the real deal. My pops says they've been like that his whole life. They won the love lottery when they found each other."

I make a note to myself to avoid seeing them kiss at all costs. I don't want to know how it ends for them.

"Now," Fifi says, "we get to work, but first we talk about clothes." She points at X. "What is horrible thing you are wearing?" She looks at him like he's a boil she wants to lance.

X looks down at himself. "What's wrong with my clothes?"

He's wearing shorts and another ironic T-shirt (it reads *Ironic T-shirt*).

"You Americans and short pants. I do not understand it."

He gives me a quick look that asks me to save him. I give him a look that says *save yourself*. "What's wrong with shorts?" he asks quite reasonably.

"Where I come from, they are for children only. Not ballroom dancing. You do not wear again."

Then she turns her attention my way and stabs me with

her eyes. I'm wearing jeans and a formless Disneyland T-shirt. "I do not know what this hobo outfit is, but will not happen again," she says.

She positions us so we're facing the floor-length mirrors. "Today we start with bachata."

X gives her his full attention. "We're doing this thing without music?" he asks.

"With those outfits, you two do not deserve music," she says.

I feel X grinning at me in the mirror, but I ignore him, admiring Fifi's outfit of the day instead. Today's asymmetrical skirt is pearl white and made from satin or silk or butter. Her stiltlike heels are scarlet. Her lipstick matches her heels.

Fifi nods at X. "I start with you," she says. "Then I do your partner and then you dance together."

"First you watch," Fifi says to X. She snaps her fingers. "One-two-three-four." Like she showed me before, she does the basic side-step, but without adding in the hip movement.

X is busy paying attention to Fifi, so I can finally let myself take a good look at him. Nothing much has changed since the last time I saw him. He's still ridiculously hot, but now that he's wearing shorts I know he has nice calves too. They're wide and muscular, with just a modicum of hair. Who even knew that I liked calves?

"Now you try," Fifi says to X, interrupting my calf musings.

His dreads are piled high again, and he rubs his hand over the back of his head. He takes a step, but with his right leg.

"No," Fifi says. "You start with left. You are lead."

"Shit. Sorry," he says, and starts again.

While he practices, Fifi quizzes him about his life. He tells her about his band (X Machine) and about where he's from (someplace called Lake Elizabeth in upstate New York).

I listen but try to make it look like I'm not listening. It involves a lot of nonchalant stretching.

He does the step a few more times before Fifi finally gives him a nod-sigh. "Good enough for now," she says, and turns back to face the mirror. "Now I show you hips." She throws me a look. "Your partner there is not so good at this part."

She repeats the side step, but this time with the infinity hips.

As soon as X begins to copy her, I drop my eyes back to the hardwood floors. I do not need to see his infinity hips.

"Fine, fine," Fifi says after a while. "Now you," she says, pointing at me.

I practice while she watches. Twice she tells me that my hips are "like rusty spring."

X cough-laughs after each insult. I glare in his general direction.

"Now you try together," Fifi says finally.

My stomach does a (small, very small) flip at the thought of standing so close to him.

"We dance open frame," Fifi says, positioning us so we're facing each other. "If we ever make it to Argentine tango, we do closed frame." She imbues the "if" with so much overwrought skepticism it sounds like *eeeeeeef*.

"Now face each other and hold hands at waist level," she says.

X takes my hands in his.

I immediately take them back. His hands are giant blocks of ice.

"Holy crap," I say. "Are you actually a corpse? Why are your hands freezing?"

"Shit, sorry!" he says. "I get cold when I'm nervous." He breathes on his hands and then rubs them together like he's trying to start a fire.

He holds out his hands again and I take them. They're not any less cold.

"Okay, now relax your shoulders. They do not belong next to ears," says Fifi, pressing on X's collarbone. "You have nice strong neck. Let the people see it."

Who are these people clamoring to see his neck? I wonder.

She turns to me, and I adjust myself under her scrutiny. My stance is perfect. But I'm holding my body so far away from his, I'm practically in another room.

"What is matter with you?" she asks me. "Is his breath stinky?"

She turns to X. "Open your mouth and breathe for me," she says.

"No way I'm doing that," he says to her without taking his eyes off me. "My breath is just fine."

I can't decide if it's basic self-respect or supreme arrogance to assert that your breath is not foul.

Fifi pokes my rib cage until I get closer to him. She adjusts us some more while explaining to X that he needs to be a strong lead.

Now that we're standing so close, he seems even taller. Which is fine. At least I don't have to look directly into his eyes. Instead, I look directly into his clavicle. It's a good word. *Clavicle.*

Fifi jerks my chin up. "Look at him," she says. "This is sexy dance, and sexy is in the eyes."

I groan, but on the inside.

"Begin," she says with a stomp of her heel.

X starts, but on the wrong foot. We go in opposite directions.

"Left foot!" says Fifi.

"Shit, sorry!" says X.

He gives me a rueful smile. A smile full of rue.

We start again with Fifi calling the count. Bachata is all about small steps, but X's are too big.

Fifi corrects him, but then he overcompensates by making them too small.

He steps on my left foot four times in a row. He says "Shit, sorry" after each foot stomp. I decide it's his favorite expression. It's possible I should wear steel-toed boots to our next practice.

Fifi moves us on to the forward basic and then to turns.

"For spot turn, lead is very important," she tells him. "You have to steer her a little bit. Let her know what you want her to do."

The first time we try it, I end up in his armpit.

"Maybe steer a little less," Fifi says, laughing. "She is not large construction vehicle."

I end up in his armpit again.

We practice without the turn for the next twenty minutes until we're both sloppy from tiredness.

"Okay, is enough for one day," says Fifi. As soon as she says it, I drop X's hands and put a few feet between us.

He frowns at me but turns to Fifi. "So you think we can win this thing?"

She scoffs. "What is expression about cart and horse?" she asks him.

"Don't put the cart before the horse," says X.

"Yes," she says, nodding. "In this case, don't bother with cart, because horse might be dead."

X catches my eye and laughs so big and deep that I can't help but laugh too.

"What is funny?" asks Fifi. "The only way to win is practice, practice, practice. I see you tomorrow. We work on other dances. Do not wear little hobo clothes again."

With her gone, the studio feels small. It gets smaller with every second that passes.

"Okay, see you," I say to X, and all but run to the closet to get my backpack.

He's right behind me when I turn around.

"My guitar's in there," he says.

I move out of his way and then move myself out of the studio and into the hall closet to get my bike. I'm just starting down the stairs when I hear him behind me.

"So how'd you get roped into this?" he asks.

I can't tell him the real truth, so I tell him the half version of it that I told Archibald and Maggie. "It sounds like fun," I say.

"You still think that even though *I'm* your partner?"

I stop in the middle of the staircase and turn to look up at him. He's three steps above me, so he's even taller than normal. "Of course. Why wouldn't I?"

"Just got the feeling you hate me a little bit."

I stumble and almost miss the final step into the outside world but manage to steady myself against my bike.

"Who said I hated you?" I say as soon as he's out on the sidewalk. The sunlight is so bright, I have to squint against it to frown at him properly.

He notices my squinting and takes a couple of steps to the right to block the sun with his head.

Thoughtful. Now I can frown at him without squinting.

"Your entire body language says you hate me," he says.

"Leave my body out of it. Look at my mouth instead."

He focuses on my mouth.

Because I just told him to.

Some days I just shouldn't speak.

I clear my throat. "What I'm saying is I don't hate you."

He holds on to his guitar straps with both hands. "Sure you do," he says.

I swing onto my bike. "I'm not going to stand here arguing with you about how much I don't hate you."

"Okay, what do you want to argue with me about, then?"

"I— What?"

He gives me that enormous brain-cell-destroying grin, and I realize he's just been teasing me this whole time.

"You're right," I say. "I do hate you."

"You don't even know me," he says.

"Yes, but once I do, I'll probably hate you."

He tilts his head to the right again. It's his thinking pose. "Oh, you can predict the future?" he asks.

I stare at him for a little too long. What would happen if I told him *Yes, I am able to predict a kind of future*?

I stand up on my pedals, getting ready to go. "Why are *you* doing this?"

"Gramps asked me to. It's a big deal for them if we win. Also, I have a *just say yes* philosophy."

"What does that mean?"

"I say yes to anything anyone asks me." At the disbelieving look on my face, he clarifies, "Nothing immoral or illegal."

"But why?"

"Life's short. Seize the day. Live in the moment," he says, smiling. "You have any philosophies I should know about?"

Does *don't banter with extremely hot and possibly smart and interesting guys who are very definitely players* count as a philosophy?

"I don't have any philosophies," I say.

"You should try the *say yes* thing. It's very freeing."

"No," I say.

"I see what you did there," he says with a smile. "I also have a *no small talk* policy."

"Why are you telling me this?"

"Just getting it all out there," he says.

I squeeze my handlebars and adjust myself on the seat. "Okay," I say, "I'm going away from you now."

"I promise to step on your toes less tomorrow," he calls out.

I pedal away and tell myself that my heart is speeding

because I'm riding so fast. Not because I was having so much fun bantering with him right there on the sidewalk. Really, I should know better than to banter. Why? Because in every romance book ever written, banter is a gateway drug. Banter leads to actual conversation, which leads to dating, which leads to kissing, which leads to coupling, which leads to heartbreak.

I turn the corner onto my street and remind myself that the only reason I'm entering this competition is so I can figure out a way to get rid of the visions. Despite how it might seem, this is not a love story.

CHAPTER 15

Dance Number Two, Excerpted

"YOU ALWAYS HAVE trouble telling left foot from right foot?"

"You are leading her, not kidnapping her!"

"Unless toes are broken, keep dancing."

"Get closer! Is his breath still stinky?"

"*Sexy* is small word. Why so difficult for you to understand?"

"No, no. Now you look like giant flightless bird. Elbows down!"

"Loose arms!"

"I danced tango with sprain ankle one time. A little toe bruise is nothing."

"No rocking side to side. You are not little teapot."

"Frame is sloppy. Why?"

"Music is privilege, not right."

CHAPTER 16

Dance Number Three

SAME AS DANCE number two but with marginally less toe bruising.

CHAPTER 17

Dance Number Four

"KEEP DANCING, I put music on now," Fifi says twenty-five minutes into our fourth practice.

I'm so shocked I miss a step.

X misses his too. "Holy shit," he says. "If we earned music, I guess we're not so bad."

"We're pretty bad," I say.

Fifi calls the bachata count—"Five-six-seven-eight"—and we begin.

Despite the music, we make our usual mistakes. The Into the Armpit Twirl™. The Toe Destroyer™.

By the third and fourth times, we make fewer mistakes.

The fifth time, we get all the footwork right.

The sixth time too.

In the middle of our seventh time, Fifi turns off the music.

"Finally, you have steps down," she says. "Now real work can begin!"

I don't know what she means by "real work," but I'm sure I don't like it.

She walks over to the closet and pulls out a boom box. Why

do we need a portable stereo when we have a perfectly functional built-in sound system? you might ask. I might ask it too.

"Evie," she says when she's done checking the boom box for batteries. "What are most important elements of ballroom?"

Despite my trepidation over what's happening with the boom box, I answer right away. "Footwork, musicality, artistry."

"Yes, but forgot two." She turns to X. "You want to guess?"

"Gotta have some bravery," he says.

"Yes, good," she says. "You must be bold. You must have showmanship." She rummages through the closet again and picks out a handful of CDs. "Last element is chemistry, but is for another time. Today we work on showmanship."

She heads for the door. "Come, come," she yells over her shoulder.

"Where are we going?" I ask.

"Come. I drive you to Santa Monica. You two are going to dance for your supper."

———

I spend the entire car ride trying to talk her out of it, but she will not be deterred. From his spot in the backseat, X is unhelpful with his silence.

I catch his eye in the rearview mirror. "Help me out," I say.

He shakes his head. "I say yes to everything, remember?"

I twist in my seat so I can face him. "You know, I thought about what you said yesterday, about living every day like it was your last."

He leans forward, interested. "Yeah?"

"I decided that it doesn't really work. If people lived like that, they would indulge all their worst impulses. They'd blow off their obligations, say and do inappropriate and immoral things, eat the wrong foods. It'd be a disaster."

He throws back his head and laughs. The sound fills up the car. "Wow, that was a dissertation. But why do you assume people would do the wrong things with their last day? Maybe they'd eat all their vegetables. Maybe they'd tell the people they love how much they love them."

I think I used to have as much faith in people as he does. I face forward. "No, they wouldn't," I say.

"All I'm saying is it could be nice to dance by the beach in front of a bunch of strangers."

"Nice or no, you're doing it," Fifi says.

Fifi parks and unearths supplies from her trunk: tip jar, boom box and CDs. Then we're on our way.

The Santa Monica promenade is basically an outdoor mall with a closed-to-traffic, paved-brick road running through it. In the spring and summer it's packed with tourists watching street performers. There are B-boy dancers, the School of Rock kids, singer/songwriter types. My absolute favorite, though, is Grumpy Clown. He looks like a desaturated version of an actual clown. If he's not stalking the length of the promenade smoking a cigarette and glowering at small children, he's sitting on one of the benches constructing the balloon animals you see in your nightmares. Seriously, they're terrifying.

Fifi chooses a spot right next to one of the dinosaur hedge-sculptures that dot the promenade.

She puts down the tip jar and seeds it with twenty dollars

from her purse. "People are more likely to like you if they think other people like you," she says to my questioning look.

X puts the boom box down next to our tip jar and Fifi loads a CD.

"Fifi—" I begin, trying to give my objections one last chance to make an impression on her.

But she's not having it. "To dance on a floor with eleven other couples, you must be fearless. You must hold judges' attention over other dancers. You must make other couples invisible."

"Fifi, man, you make it sound like we're going to war," X says.

"It *is* war," she says. "And right now you are not good weapon." She claps her hands together. "Into position."

I take two deep breaths to calm myself. The air's a mix of ocean brine, floral perfumes and that new-leather mall smell. The almost-lunchtime sun is high and hot. It feels like a spotlight shining down on us.

"I start you off easy," Fifi says, and stoops to press play on the CD.

At first, we're Tin-Man-from-Wizard-of-Oz stiff. I'm hyper-self-conscious and, paradoxically, hyperaware of everyone walking by. I sneak a peek at our potential "audience." We get vaguely curious glances from tourists. The locals—the people who actually work nearby and are used to all kinds of performances—ignore us completely.

Next to us, Fifi hisses corrections: "Infinity hips! Stronger frame! Eye contact!"

The first song ends, but Fifi doesn't give us time to rest. She plays three more bachata songs in a row. The tempo increases with each, so that by the fourth I'm concentrating too hard to have time for self-consciousness.

By the time the last song ends fifteen minutes later, X and I are both breathing hard.

Fifi waves us over. "Tell me," she says. "Why you think no one is watching?"

I don't answer. I know a rhetorical question when I hear one.

Evidently, X does too, because he doesn't answer either.

"Not watching because both of you dancing with head, not heart. And too busy paying attention to the people not paying attention to you." She looks at X. "You are in band. You perform on stage. Where is boldness?"

"Singing and ballroom dancing are not the same thing, Fi," he says.

"But you have to have charisma, yes? Where is charisma?" she asks.

She turns to me. "Technique is not terrible," she says. "But you are smoke without fire."

I'm sure she's right. Still I want to point out that

    a) smoke is very hot

and

    b) people die just as much from smoke inhalation
       as they do from actual flames.

However, there's no way saying any of that will help my case.

Some little kids climb onto the wall surrounding the dinosaur sculptures and start pretending to be dinosaurs. They roar and I kind of want to join them.

"Try again," Fifi says.

X and I move back into position.

"Let down your braids," he says.

I touch my hand to my high ponytail and frown at him. "Why?"

"Just say yes," he says. "We're letting it all hang out."

Something about taking my hair down feels too intimate. It makes me shy and unsteady.

"You have to take your dreads down too, then," I say, trying to get my footing back.

He pulls out his hair tie with one hand. His locs fall around his shoulders and frame his face.

Our eyes meet and there's a thread of something—an extra awareness—between us. A small, unwise part of me wants to hold on to that thread and see where it leads. The larger, more sensible part of me wants to find huge metaphorical scissors and snip that thread into tiny pieces.

The next song begins. Maybe it's because our hair is down or because Fifi basically dared us to stop sucking, but for whatever reason, this dance is different.

The singer is a crooner. His voice sounds like he's just found the meaning of life and he's about to tell you what it is. Beneath his voice, the 4/4 rhythm is insistent. X throws his shoulders back and smiles into my eyes. His lead is confident. Somehow my hips have unsprung. Infinity hips achieved.

We slip into another song and then another. By the time we stop, there's a crowd of fifteen or twenty people around us. Some of them even walk over to drop money into our tip jar.

I wait for them to drift away before I count up our earnings. "There's fifty-seven dollars in here," I say, shocked.

"Minus Fifi's twenty, that's thirty-seven bucks in forty minutes," X adds.

That's pretty good, actually.

"So how'd we look, Fi?" X asks.

I know we danced those last songs better than we ever have, but that doesn't mean it was actually any good.

Fifi is uncharacteristically quiet.

"You're scaring me," I tell her.

"Me too," says X.

"It's still early stages," she says.

"Yes," I agree.

She turns to me. "And hips are better, but still nonsense."

"Okay," I say.

She turns to X. "And you couldn't lead a cow to grass."

He just laughs.

"But maybe together you might have something," she says smiling.

"Mostly me, though, right?" X says.

"Definitely," she says.

"Hey," I say, "just because he's hot—"

X's head whips around. "You think I'm hot?"

Gobsmacked is the word I'd use to describe his face.

In situations like this, most people wish for a hole to open up and swallow them into the ground. But I don't want that. What I want is to *be the hole*. I don't know what that sentiment means, but I'm sure I mean it.

"I meant to say *she* thinks you're hot," I say, stabbing my finger at Fifi.

Fifi cocks her head and stares at us the way you'd look at a piece of art you don't quite understand in a museum. "Huh," she says.

"What?" I ask.

"Finally, I understand what problem is."

"Great. Maybe you could tell me," X says.

"Never mind problem," she says. "I have solution. Tomorrow instead of practice, you two go out and get to know each other."

"We're fine—" I begin.

"Not fine," she counters. "One of most important elements of ballroom is chemistry. Go out and get to be friends."

Put like that, it almost sounds reasonable.

X grins. "Yes, whatever it takes," he says, because, annoyingly, he says yes to everything.

Of course I have to agree too.

We dance three more dances and earn another eighteen dollars.

Fifi takes a ten-percent cut.

Back at the studio, X and I exchange phone numbers before going our separate ways.

———

There's a subgenre of romance books I like to call Shipwrecked. In them, the unsuspecting (and usually feuding) main characters are somehow forced to spend enough time together that they realize how much they like spending time together. For example, the couple is trapped in a (small, romantic) cabin in the woods because of a snowstorm. Or the couple is stranded on a (beautiful, tropical, not-at-all-dangerous) deserted island because of stormy seas.

What I'm saying is that Fifi is a storm, X and I are the unsuspecting main characters, and us getting to know each other for the sake of dance chemistry is a small cabin in a snowy wood.

CHAPTER 18

A Strict Definition

Sophie, "Me," Cassidy and Martin >

Sophie: So what you're saying is you're going on a date with the sexy new guy you met at your sexy new hobby. Do I have that right?

Me: It's not a date

Sophie: I'm using the strict definition of the word

Cassidy: Which is what?

Sophie: Two or more people meeting at a fixed location at an appointed time for a predetermined reason

Martin: Where are you going?

Me: Ughhhh

Me: Ughhhhhhhhh

Me: He wants to go on one of those celebrity tours

Martin: Ew

Me: Right?!

Sophie: I've always wanted to go on one of those

Cassidy: Rlly? didn't think u'd b in 2 that

Sophie: What? I can be shallow

Cassidy: I like that ur not shallow

Me: Are you guys flirting? It feels like you're flirting

Cassidy: We r not flirting

Sophie: Exactly

Me: ANYWAY

———

Sophie and "Me" >

Sophie: Why'd you say that thing about Cassidy flirting with me

Me: I was just kidding

Me: Why?

Me: Do you want her to flirt with you?

Sophie: Of course not

Sophie: It was just a weird thing for you to say

———

Cassidy and "Me" >

Cassidy: No tongue on the 1st date

Me: Shut.

Me: Up.

———

Martin and "Me" >

Me: I think something's up with them

Martin: Yeah, maybe

Me: I blame spring

Me: It's like the pollen makes people extra kissy

Martin: You're saying kissing is an allergic reaction?

Me: For which there is no cure

———

CHAPTER 19

❀

Not a Date, Part 1 of 3

I GET TO LaLaLand Tours with fifteen minutes to spare. The office is in a strip mall with a pawn shop on one side, a check cashing place on the other and Hollywood Walk of Fame stars stenciled into the sidewalk in front. Irony, thy name is Hollywood.

As soon as I walk in, a pretty but entirely too-animated young white woman holding a clipboard and wearing a *LaLaLand Tours* T-shirt hands me a sheet of paper. On one side is an FAQ with a prominent disclaimer reminding us that we are not guaranteed to see celebrities frolicking in their natural habitat on this tour.

X walks in ten minutes after when we said we'd meet. I think one side effect of living in the moment is that it makes you late for appointments. As usual, his dreads are up high on his head. He's wearing skinny black jeans, a short-sleeved white button-down and blue floral canvas sneakers. I watch him move about the room and realize I'm not the only one watching him. Besides his looks, there's something compelling about him. Maybe it's the openness of his face? Or the way he seems so interested in the world, like right here, right now is exactly where he wants to be.

Pretty clipboard woman hands him his FAQ/disclaimer.

He flashes his absurdly beautiful smile at her.

She takes off all her clothes.

I'm kidding.

She doesn't do that.

But she wants to.

"X," I call out to him so she knows he's actually meeting someone here.

Clipboard lady gets everyone's attention and shepherds us all outside. The bus is an open-air double-decker behemoth festooned with pictures of famous landmarks and grainy photos of surprised, not-entirely-pleased-looking celebrities.

"Upper or lower deck?" X asks.

I choose upper. It's a nice day and just overcast enough that we won't bake in the sun.

"How many of these tours have you been on?" he asks as we climb the stairs.

"None," I say.

"Really?"

"I'm from here," I remind him.

"All the more reason," he says.

The first half of the tour is, to my surprise, pretty interesting. Even though we don't see any celebrities, our guide tells us funny stories about previous sightings. There was one famous reality TV star who they caught picking his nose when the tour bus pulled up next to his car. She doesn't say who the star was but gives us enough clues to figure it out.

When we hit Sunset Strip, X turns to me with an *are you seeing what I'm seeing?* look on his face.

"What?" I ask.

"That's the Roxy," he says. "And Whisky a Go Go." Both the Roxy and Whisky a Go Go are famous nightclubs. He says the names with such reverence that I can't help feeling a little excited for him.

I look out at them, but I know that where I'm just seeing another average building, he's seeing history.

"You haven't gone yet?" I ask.

"Not yet," he says. He gets out his phone and starts taking pictures. "Man, you know what kind of legends played the Roxy? Bob Marley and the Wailers. George Benson. Jane's Addiction. The Doors were Whisky a Go Go's house band for a while."

I look back out at the buildings, already starting to see them differently. "So your dream is to play there?" I ask.

"I'll get there," he says.

"Are you always so . . . confident?"

"You were going to say 'cocky,' weren't you?"

"No," I lie.

He gives me an *I don't believe you at all* smile.

It's a nice smile. I move us on from it. "You want to be a musician?"

He shifts position so he can face me better. "We're really doing this thing?"

"What thing?"

"What Fifi told us to do. The get-to-know-each-other thing."

"If there was a ballroom dance mafia, Fifi would be the kingpin. Our lives will be easier if we just do what she says."

"I feel you," he says with a quick laugh. He looks back at the clubs as we pass them. "I'm a musician already. What I want is to be a rock star. I want world domination. I want the big stadium. The sold-out shows. The cover of *Rolling Stone*. The induction into the Rock and Roll Hall of Fame."

"The groupies," I interject.

He laughs and shrugs.

"But the odds are so against you," I say.

"Yeah, so I've heard." He sounds defiant and tired at the same time.

I'm sure I'm not the first person to tell him that his probability of making it is low. I wonder how his parents feel about his big dream. Parents don't usually love it when their kids take risks with their futures.

"You know what, though?" I say. "If everybody thought about the odds, there'd be no rock stars in the first place."

His smile comes back, and I'm happier about it than I probably should be.

Our bus pulls up to a stoplight. A few pedestrians wave like *we're* the actual celebrities.

"So you moved out here to become a rock star?"

"That's part of it."

"What's the other part?"

He examines my face for a few seconds. I get the feeling he's trying to decide how much to trust me with. "A friend of mine died last year. Clay. He was our bassist."

"Oh, X, I'm so sorry."

He nods down at his hands. "Me too."

I don't think he's going to say anything else, but then he

does. "The band was me, Clay, Jamal on drums and Kevin on keys. We almost called ourselves The Lonely Onlys."

"How come?"

"Not a whole lot of Black kids in the Lake Elizabeth school system," he says with a smile. "Clay and I knew each other from middle school. We met Kevin and Jamal at band tryout freshman year of high school. We said it was a miracle that there were four of us." The memory of the day is in his eyes. "And before you give me a hard time again, I didn't pick the name X Machine myself."

"When did I give you a hard time?"

"Seriously? You don't remember? When we first met. Your exact words were 'So the band is named after you?'"

"Are you sure?" I ask, even though I remember perfectly. "That doesn't sound like me."

"You have an evil twin sister?"

"No."

"Then it was you."

We grin at each other.

"Clay came up with the name. He said since I was front man and the band was my idea, it was only right. We all thought X Machine sounded like we were from the future." He drops his head back against the headrest. He swallows once and then twice, like he's trying to hold down something that wants to come out. "It happened so fast. One minute he was there, and the next he was gone."

Now I get it. I understand why he says yes to everything and why he tries to live in the moment. It's because his friend died. He's not being pretentious, like I thought he was. Like

I *hoped* he was. He's smart and thoughtful and funny, maybe even a little philosophical.

I need for him to be altogether less . . . everything.

I need for him to have a secret stash of toenail clippings or nose hairs.

The bus makes a wide left turn. I slide along the seat and my shoulder presses into his. I have to wait for the turn to end before I can pull away again.

"We were planning to move out here after high school anyway. After Clay died, me and the guys decided to seize the day. We dropped out of high school."

"Wait. You dropped out of high school?"

"Yeah."

"But aren't you a senior? You only had one semester to go."

"Some things can't wait, Evie."

"Is that why you broke up with Jess?" I ask. "To move out here and become a rock star?"

"Wow, I'm surprised you remember her name," he says.

"I have a good memory for names," I say. I mean, I don't actually, but it's better if he thinks I do.

"Jess and I weren't going to work out. We didn't fit."

There's so much I want to ask about why they didn't fit, but I definitely should not be delving into his love life. Now's a good time for a topic switch, I decide.

"How do your parents feel about you dropping out of school?"

"Poorly," he says. He turns to look at me. "You ever wanted something so bad you couldn't wait?"

"Yeah," I say, but I don't elaborate. The day I rode from

school all the way to Santa Monica to try to convince Dad to come home was the most I've ever wanted anything.

We spend the rest of the tour mostly lost in our own thoughts. "Sorry we didn't see any stars," I say as we're getting off the bus.

"No worries. Still got something out of it."

"What?"

"We did the assignment and got to know each other a little."

Fifi. Right. I kind of lost sight of the reason we were hanging out in the first place.

"We might even become friends," he says.

"Fifi said we had to get to know each other, not like each other," I say, teasing.

"Yeah, but you like me. I can tell."

"Have you ever heard the expression 'She rolled her eyes so hard she saw her own brain'?"

He slaps his hand to his chest and laughs a loud, wide-open laugh. It's a great laugh.

"Can we at least agree that you don't hate me?" he asks.

"I don't hate you," I say.

He throws an arm around me and grins. "Well, that's a start," he says.

CHAPTER 20

By Act Two

Sophie, "Me," Cassidy and Martin >

Sophie: Wow, another date?

Me: It. Is. Not. A. Date

Cassidy: Lemme get this straight. The v hot rocker invited u 2 c him play his guitar & sing his songs with his band @ his v first gig in LA?

Martin: Jesus, Cassidy, would it kill you to write the words out? I just had to read that five times

Cassidy: F U

Cassidy: Anyway

Cassidy: How hot is he exactly?

Me: You don't even like boys

Cassidy: Rockstars r not boys. They're not even human. They're a separate species

Martin: Truth

Me: We're just going out to get to know each other

Cassidy: Rt. So u can have bttr chemistry when ur dirty dancing with each other

Me: BALLROOM DANCING IS NOT THE SAME AS DIRTY DANCING

Cassidy: Come on. It's sex with clothes on

Martin: Truth

Sophie: Omg, Cassidy

Cassidy: What?

Cassidy: She's basically the heroine in 1 of her romance books

Martin: She doesn't read those books anymore

Cassidy: She'll be in love by the end of act 2

Me: You understand that real life doesn't have acts, right?

Martin: Truth

———————

CHAPTER 21

Not a Date, Part 2 of 3

THE CLUB WHERE X is playing is a hole in the wall. With no windows. And very dim light. A cave, basically.

I peer into the near darkness from the doorway, wishing for a spelunking helmet, which is not something I've ever wished for before. I don't see X, but our plan was that I'd watch the show and we'd meet up afterward.

So far only a handful of people are here, some at the bar and a few others at the tables in the back. At the front of the room, a small elevated stage is already set up. I spot an electric guitar with an *X Machine* sticker leaning up against an amp. I can't believe he's really going to get up there and sing and play in front of a bunch of strangers. I can't believe how nervous I am for him.

I look away from the stage, suck in a deep breath and immediately cough that deep breath back out. The air smells like smoke, beer, pee and the cleaning products they use to (unsuccessfully) cover the smell of smoke, beer and pee. I choose a table as far away from the stage as I can find. I don't want my nervousness to make him nervous. Not that it would. But still, to be safe.

The show's supposed to start at six, but (by law) rock shows are not allowed to start on time. People trickle in over the next forty minutes until the club is packed. Finally, a short white Mohawked guy dressed all in black leather goes up to the mic. His skin, including his face, is almost entirely covered with tattoos.

"Welcome to Ricky's Club," he says in a thick English accent. "I'm Ricky. We got a good show for you tonight. First up, X Machine, all the way from—"

He stops talking and yells backstage. "Where are you lot from, again?"

"Lake Elizabeth," yells a voice.

"Right," says Ricky. "Lake Elizabeth." He looks backstage again. "Where the fuck is that, then?"

"Upstate New York," says the same voice.

Ricky faces the audience. "There you go," he says. "Upstate fucking New York."

I watch the crowd, trying to gauge their enthusiasm. It is tepid.

My nervousness spikes. I really want him to be good. Not just good, but great. As great as he thinks he is. I don't want this impossible dream to break his heart.

Before he leaves the stage, Ricky announces the band that X Machine is opening for—"hometown favorites Better Daze." The crowd reaction is not tepid. Probably half the audience are friends of theirs, but enthusiasm is enthusiasm.

The house lights dim even more and all three guys walk out onstage. I remember a little about them from our LaLaLand tour. Jamal's the drummer and Kevin's the bassist. Kevin used to play keys, but he started playing bass after Clay died.

X picks up the electric guitar and walks to the mic. Up there he looks different somehow. Maybe it's because his dreads are loose around his shoulders. Or maybe it's the way the stage lights make his brown skin glow slightly blue. His eyes search the crowd. It takes me a second to realize he's looking for me. I throw my hand into the air and wave.

He waves back and a few people in the audience turn to look at me.

"Hey, everyone," he says into the mic. His voice is deeper than I'm used to. "We're X Machine. We're from Upstate fucking New York. This is our first gig in LA. Thanks for coming out. This song is called 'Prom.'"

In classic rock-and-roll-drummer fashion, Jamal slaps his sticks together and calls the count. "One, two, three, four."

I expect—and the audience expects—a hard, driving tempo, but that's not what we get. The song is slow. Too slow.

X's voice is too melting smooth. He's basically crooning over the midtempo rhythm. The lyrics are too sweet and earnest—something about corsages and promises.

One of Dad's favorite sayings is *don't bring a knife to a gunfight.* All I can think now is don't bring a ballad to a rock concert. The audience starts to fidget.

But then they launch into the chorus, and the whole song changes. X's voice takes on an edge—not angry, but hard. The tempo increases.

> *I don't wanna go*
> *I don't wanna go*
> *I don't wanna go to prom with you*

The rest of the song is pretty much about everything that's wrong with prom—the tulle, the bow ties, the crappy music, the pressure to make out and move around the bases, the unrealistic expectations that you'll one day marry your prom date. It's hilarious and catchy, and by the end everyone is hating on prom right along with them.

"That beginning fake-out always fools people," X says after the applause dies down. "This next song is called 'Race Is Stupid.'"

This one doesn't start off slow or crooning. The song is rage set to music and still catchy somehow. I already know the chorus will stay with me:

> *You don't get to say*
> *Who I am*
> *Who I can be*
> *You don't get to tell me*
> *Nothing no more*
> *Nothing no more*
> *Nothing*

They play two more songs, and I can't take my eyes off him. Let's just say I get why rock stars are a thing. I get why groupies are a thing. Because up there onstage with his guitar, X's sexy is undeniable. But what really gets me is the way I can see he belongs up there. It's the way he doesn't hold anything back.

He pulls the mic in close. "Here's a brand-new one we started working on last night. The lyrics aren't all there yet, but it's got potential. See what you guys think," he says.

He unstraps his guitar and leans it up against the wall.

"This song is called 'Black Box,'" he says, and grips the mic stand with both hands.

The bass and drums kick in before X does. His voice, when it comes, is low and sprawling and full of so much want that it doesn't matter that he's mumble-singing some of the lyrics. At the chorus, he grips the mic stand and tilts it forward like he needs more room for his voice to grow, like he needs more room for the feeling he's trying to give us all to grow.

An idea of what his future will be like rises in my mind. Not a tiny club, but a stadium. Not fifty people, but fifty thousand. Not an unfinished song, but a catalog of hits. In this future, he gets everything he wants. But then I shake my head, because of course, it probably won't happen that way. Over the last few weeks with the visions, I've seen enough heartbreak to know that life almost never turns out the way you think it will.

The song ends and X grips the mic again. "I know it's weird for you seeing three Black guys up here playing rock and roll. But don't forget, Black people invented rock and roll." He winks and flashes the same grin he gave me when we first met, the one that gets him to the front of every line. It works, and people laugh all around me. He waits for the cheers to die down. "We're X Machine. That was our set," he says. "Thanks for coming out."

The club lights go up from dark to slightly less dark.

It's another twenty minutes of breaking down their equipment and high fives and *great show*s before he makes his way over to me. He brings Jamal and Kevin with him.

"You the one got our boy doing ballet?" Jamal asks. He's taller than X, with a baby face and a Mohawk.

"That's me," I say.

"Man, I told you it's not ballet. It's ballroom," X groans. I can tell this is a running gag between them.

Jamal gives me a quick hug. "Keep him busy with the dancing," he says. "Before you, he was killing us with rehearsing all the time."

"He's a lot less grumpy now too," Kevin says, also leaning in for a hug. He's short, wide and completely bald. In a former life he was a boulder.

"Time for you fools to go," X says.

Jamal laughs. "Nice to meet you finally, Evie," he says.

"Keep up the good work," Kevin adds.

After they leave, X turns back to me. "Hey," he says. His eyes are glittering, and there's a kind of energy coursing through him.

I grab my backpack and hug it tight to my chest. "Hey," I say back. And even at the risk of seeming like a groupie, I have to tell him how great he was. "You were incredible. Better than you said you were. Thanks for inviting me. I'm glad I got to see you play."

He beams. Which isn't something I've seen him do before, but I like it. I like it so much that I want to make him do it again.

———

"This place isn't usually like this," I say to X when we're settled into our booth at Surf City Waffle. I've never actually been here at night, and it's . . . different. The tables are covered with lacey, pale-pink cloths. Rose petals float in small round vases at the center of each table. Actual candles in actual sconces line the walls. Candlelight twinkles. Romantically.

X makes a show of looking around. "So you didn't bring me here to seduce me?" he asks.

I actually sputter. "What?! No!"

He leans back and belly-laughs with his giant hands resting on his stomach. "Got your goat," he says.

"Leave my goat alone," I grumble.

"Don't make it so easy to catch, then," he says. His dreads are half in his face.

"Also, you shouldn't flirt with me. I'm not one of your groupies."

He does the single-eyebrow-raise thing. "Who says I'm flirting?"

"My flirt-detection meter," I say.

He leans forward. "Where do you get one of those?"

"Same place I got my bullshit-detection meter," I say, leaning back into my seat.

Another belly laugh from him. "You're funny," he says.

"I bet you flirt with everyone," I say.

He shakes his head. "Not everyone."

I persist. "But you flirt a lot, right?"

"I like girls," he says. He turns the vase centerpiece idly with his long fingers. "I especially like the smart, pretty, snarky, slightly confusing ones."

"Too bad there aren't any of those around," I say.

Then I remind myself that he's probably had no less than ten thousand girlfriends. I wonder if he's ever loved any of them, if he's ever had his heart broken. I know for sure he broke Jess's heart while cycling my bike around studio five.

Like I should've done several sentences ago, I change the subject. "What was that last song you played? The one that's not finished yet?"

Before he can answer, the waitress drops off our food. Chicken and waffles for him. Waffle with berries for me.

He bites into his chicken. "Damn, that's good." He devours it in about two minutes flat. "Sorry," he says, leaning back and wiping his hands. "Being onstage makes me hungry." He watches me construct the perfect forkful of waffle, strawberry syrup and whipped cream.

I pull my plate in closer. "Don't even look at my food," I warn him.

"Don't worry, I'm good now," he says, leaning back. "The last song was 'Black Box.'"

"What's it about?"

"A lot of things. But mostly my pops. We used to be close, but things have been messed up with us since Clay died. I don't see the world the same way I used to, and now it's like we can't understand each other anymore." His voice is a mixture of regret and confusion and anger.

"What happened?"

"We don't agree on the direction of my future," he says, using a deep, imperious voice, like a judge pronouncing a verdict.

I take a guess. "He doesn't want you to be a musician."

"He says it's fine for a hobby." He picks up his fork, drags it across his plate and then puts it back down. "The messed-up thing is, *he's* the one who got me my first guitar. *He* gave me my first lessons. We even had our own band when I was little."

"You did?" I picture a younger version of X, which is basically the same as this version of X except shorter and rounder and with smaller hands.

"We called ourselves the WoodsMen. Get it? Because my last name is—"

I interrupt him. "Xavier Woods, I'm not an idiot."

"My middle name is Darius," he says, grinning. "I'm telling you so you can yell my full name when you're yelling at me."

"Thanks, that's very thoughtful of you, Xavier Darius Woods," I say, laughing.

"Anyway, me and Pops would do these little concerts for the rest of the family at Thanksgiving and Christmas and stuff."

"What kind of music?"

"I like to think we defied genre labels," he says.

"That means you were terrible, doesn't it?"

He laughs. "Worse than terrible."

A waitress comes over and refills our water glasses.

"Sorry, didn't mean to bring us down with all that about my pops," he says after she leaves.

"No, it's okay. I know how you feel. I used to be close to my dad too."

"Yeah? What happened with you guys?"

I hesitate. The only other people who know about this are Martin, Sophie and Cassidy.

"No worries if you don't want to get into it with me," he

says. But I do want to talk about it with him. He knows what it's like to miss the way things used to be.

"He cheated on my mom and I caught him doing it."

He sits up straight. "Jesus, Evie."

I tell him the whole story. It's hard to look at him and talk about it, so I look down at my plate instead. "Anyway, it's been around six months since I last saw him."

"Does your mom know?"

"Yeah, but my sister doesn't."

"Jesus," he says again, but quietly.

"The weirdest thing is, Mom and Danica both seem fine. It's like this big bomb went off in our lives and I'm the only one who got hurt."

I make myself look up at him. His eyes are full of understanding. "Well," he says, "I still think I win the sad story contest."

At first I'm too shocked to react. That is not what I expected him to say. I expected sympathy and comforting. I didn't expect him to judge how sad my story was against his.

He busts out laughing, and then I do too.

After a while we stop laughing, but our eyes meet and the moment lingers until I realize what's happening and look away. "Why don't you sing the song for me?" I ask.

He looks confused for a second but then pulls out his phone and plays the backing music track.

He starts singing. *"Everything burns / Everything crashes / And some-thing some-thing some-other-thing."* He stops with a laugh. "I don't know that third line yet," he says.

"You're very good at mumble-singing, though," I say. "You just need something to rhyme with *crashes*." I twirl my braids around my finger and think until a line comes to me. "And our love just turns to ashes," I say.

"Oh, that's good." He types it into his phone and looks back up at me. "All right, the next line slows the tempo way down, but I only have half of it. "You're the black box, some-thing, some-other-thing—"

"Falling to the sea," I say, interrupting him again.

"Good, good," he says, typing fast. He leans forward, eyes glittering. "Let's keep going."

"Okay, but we need actual paper instead of just your phone."

I ask the waitress and she brings us over a few sheets and a pen. He writes down what we have so far and then keeps sing-ing. "A black box, preserving history."

I shake my head. "*One last* history, instead of *preserving* history."

He writes it down.

Both of us are grinning now, trading the pen and paper back and forth. By the time we get to the end, the sheet is a mess of crossed-out words and arrows pointing every which way.

"Wish I had my acoustic," he says, pulling the sheet closer. On the phone, he restarts the backing music track and sings the whole thing.

I close my eyes so I can really listen and not be distracted by his face. It's strange but nice to hear his voice singing words we just wrote together. Somehow when he sings the words they gain more weight. It makes them feel more true. When he gets to the final three lines, my eyes fly open. His voice is so raw, so filled with wishing for something he can't have back, that I have to see his face.

"You're great," he says. "At writing songs, I mean." He rubs his hand over the back of his head.

"We wrote it together."

"I've never written a song with another person before," he says. "Not even Clay." He shakes the sheet of paper at me. "Can I use these?"

"They're already yours. You helped write them."

"It was mostly you," he says.

I shrug. "I'm really good at understanding heartbreak. It's my superpower."

CHAPTER 22

"Black Box," Lyrics by Evie Thomas and Xavier Woods

[Verse 1]

Everything burns
Everything crashes
And our love just turns to ashes
You're a black box, falling to the sea
A black box, one last history

[Chorus]

Open you up
Look inside
Already know
Just what I'll find
Nothing survives
Nothing survives
Nothing survives

[Verse 2]

The you that I knew
Sinks down out of sight
I'm left with nothing

And yeah nothing is fucking all right
Black box, at the bottom of the sea

[Chorus]
Open you up
Look inside
Already know
Just what I'll find
Nothing survives
Nothing survives
Nothing survives

[Bridge]
It's all in my head
Just an illusion I said
And know that you're gone
Everything is all so beautifully wrong
All wrong, all wrong, all wrong

[Chorus]
Open you up
Look inside
Already know
Just what I'll find
Nothing survives
Nothing survives
Nothing survives

CHAPTER 23

Fabulous, Excellent and Copacetic

"Me," Martin, Cassidy and Sophie >

Me: I invited X to our bonfire tonight

Martin: Okay

Cassidy: K

Sophie: Ok

Me: Huh

Me: You guys don't have anything else to say?

Cassidy: Nope

Cassidy: Why?

Cassidy: U have sumthing else 2 say?

Me: Nope

Cassidy: Fabulous

Martin: Excellent

Sophie: Copacetic

Me: I don't even like you people

CHAPTER 24

Not a Date, Part 3 of 3

DOCKWEILER STATE BEACH is one of my favorite places in the world. The beach itself is beautiful, with wide stretches of (mostly clean) sand and an always-churning dark-blue ocean that seems to fall off the end of the world. There's a bicycle path and a picnic area and even showers. My favorite part, though, are the fire rings that line the beach. If you get here early enough, you can claim one and have a bonfire with your friends underneath a darkening sky while listening to the Pacific crash all around you. It might be the most perfect place on earth.

"Is that him?" Cassidy asks.

I look up from the fire pit to see X wobbling across the sand.

"It's easier if you take off your shoes," I yell to him.

He stops to take them off and then wobbles a slightly steadier wobble toward us.

"You're X," Cassidy says when he gets to us. "Evie's friend."

I don't know if I'm imagining the small pause between "Evie's" and "friend."

"I'm Cassidy," she says. "I'm the rich, wild, parentally neglected friend. I got you booze." She picks up one of the five bottles of white wine she brought. Earlier when I told her we didn't need that many, she said, "My parents won't even notice they're missing."

"I'm Martin. I guess I'm the sensitive one," Martin says to X. "I got you a chair." He points to the beach chair nestled in the sand next to mine.

"And I'm Sophie," Sophie chimes in. "I'm the steady, boring one," she says.

Cassidy takes a sip of wine. "You're not boring," she says.

"Thanks," Sophie says, smiling. She turns back to X. "I brought you the most delicious sandwich in all of Los Angeles."

X waves. "Thanks for letting me crash."

"Evie says you're incredible," Cassidy says.

X's eyebrows shoot up.

I rush to clarify. "Incredible at making music. What Cassidy means is that I said you're an incredible musician."

"Yes," says Cassidy, looking back and forth between us with a gleeful smile on her face. "That's exactly what I meant."

I give her a look at says *no one will find your dismembered, fish-gnawed body at the bottom of the sea.*

She ignores me. "Anyway, you can play to thank us. Every good bonfire needs a hot guy playing guitar."

"You don't have to play," I tell him.

"But you still have to be hot," Cassidy says.

"I don't mind doing both," he says with a grin.

Martin tells him to sit.

Sophie tells him to eat.

Cassidy hands him an almost overflowing cup of wine.

Instead of sitting with everyone, I tend the fire. I'm the group fire starter because I'm the only one who's good at it. I learned my technique—crumpled newspaper nestled under a shallow, three-log pyramid—from Dad. The four of us used to come here at least once a week every "winter." The quotes around *winter* are Dad's. He's originally from Washington, DC, where winter is a real season, with snow and ice and weather-induced tears. Here in LA, the temperature rarely drops below fifty. When it does, it's just an excuse for us to wear fashionable scarves and sheepskin boots and pretend to be cold for a few days. Dad loved our bonfires because the beach at night in winter is the coldest LA ever gets. It reminded him of home.

The last time the four of were together out here was a few months before Mom and Dad told us they were getting divorced. If I'd known it was going to be the last time, I'd have memorized all the details. All I remember now are probablys.

Probably Mom made a stew, oxtail or beef, and packed Tupperwares for each of us. Probably Dad poked at the fire obsessively. Probably we all laughed and called him a pyromaniac. At some point, he and Mom would've started drinking wine, and they'd have laughed more and touched each other more. Probably they told embarrassing stories about when Danica and I were toddlers. Probably Danica and I smiled at each other in the firelight and pretended to be embarrassed. The next day, we probably all smelled like smoke and stew and ocean. I'm sure we found sand in our clothes.

"Everything good?" X calls to me from his beach chair. He's really more observant than he needs to be.

"Yeah," I say, and just like Dad, I poke at the logs, which absolutely don't need any poking.

"Pyromaniac," X says.

It's the perfect night for a bonfire. The temperature is just right—cold enough that you want to sit next to fire, but not so cold that you'd rather be *in* the fire. Even the wind is cooperating, swirling so gently that smoke drifts straight up into the air instead of gusting sideways into our faces.

I toss another log on and listen while the four of them chat a get-to-know-you chat. X tells them where he's from and about his band and about dropping out of high school. Cassidy is really impressed with that last part.

I try not to watch X as he talks, but I can't help myself. Firelight flickers across his face and lights him up. He does a lot of grinning and chuckling. I decide I like people who are generous with their laughter.

Once X realizes the three of us have been friends since middle school, he begs for funny—meaning embarrassing—stories about me. I threaten to douse the fire. Cassidy declares herself impervious to cold. She tells him the story of when I peed on myself while running up a very long staircase in first grade. X laughs and tells the story of how he peed on himself on the school bus in second grade and how he sat and waited until everyone was off the bus before getting off and running all the way back home.

Eventually we get to the Tipsy Philosophicals portion of the evening. This is when we're all just tipsy enough to ask and answer pseudo-philosophical questions. We're allowed at most once short sentence to explain ourselves. We can answer "I don't know" only once.

Martin starts us off: Is seven years too long a time to be unrequitedly in love with someone?

> **Martin:** No amount of time is too long for true love.
> **Me:** Yes, especially if that someone is related to your best friend.
> **Cassidy:** All my loves have always been requited.
> **Sophie:** Yes, unfortunately.
> **X:** Yeah, I don't know, but I think I might be finding out soon.

I'm next: If you could find out when and how you were going to die, would you?

> **Martin:** No.
> **Cassidy:** Nooooooo.
> **Sophie:** No.
> **X:** No way. Imagine all the dread you'd feel waiting for it to happen. It'd take the fun out of being alive.
> **Me:** Yes, it's always good to be prepared.

Next is Cassidy: Is unconditional love real?

> **Martin:** Of course.
> **Cassidy:** Absolutely not.

Sophie: Yes.

X: Yeah, for sure.

Me: No, and also shouldn't there be conditions?

Then Sophie: Is there such a thing as happily ever after?

Martin: Yes.

Cassidy: No.

Sophie: Yes.

X: Absolutely yes.

Me: How long is Ever, and when is After? What I'm saying is "no."

And finally, X: Is there life after death?

Martin: I don't know.

Cassidy: God, I hope not.

Sophie: No, not according to science.

X: I don't know, but I hope so.

Me: I don't know and I don't want to know.

We play a few more rounds. Martin asks if love can last forever. Cassidy and I are the only ones who say that it can't. Cassidy is just being her ornery, cynical self.

I, on the other hand, have actual proof that it doesn't.

Despite our rule about not getting into long-winded discussions about the answers, we do anyway. X can't believe that I'd want to know where and when I was going to die. "It'd be terrible," he says. "You'd have a huge existential cloud of doom hovering over your head all the time."

Everyone gives Cassidy a hard time for saying she hopes there's no life after death. "Once is enough for me, thank you very much," she says. Eventually, though, she relents and says it'd be okay if she "ends up where all the cool, fun people are." It's not clear to any of us if she thinks that's heaven or hell or someplace else.

After a while we move on to gossiping about our classmates, which means we gossip about their love lives. I know for certain that the next topic will be our own love lives.

I'm not sure I'm ready to hear how active X's has been. "I have to pee," I say, too loud from tipsiness.

"I'll walk you," Martin says, as he always does. The bathroom is too far away and too isolated for us to go alone, so we use the buddy system. Martin's always the buddy.

"I need to go too," says X.

Martin sits back down and winks at me.

We walk along for a little while, not saying anything until X breaks the silence.

"I like your friends. Thanks for inviting me."

"They like you too."

"Cassidy is pretty funny."

"Yeah, it's too bad her parents suck."

"Did she and Sophie ever used to go out?"

"No . . . why?"

He shrugs. "No reason. They seem close, is all."

"We're *all* pretty close. We survived the orgy of awkwardness that is middle school together. We're bonded for life, like war soldiers."

He laughs. "So you were awkward in middle school?" he asks.

"Wasn't everyone?"

"Nah, I've always been this cool."

"You're not that cool," I say, but neither of us believes I mean it.

We get to the restroom and stand guard for each other before making our way back.

It really *is* a perfect night. One of those that make me feel lucky I get to live in a place as beautiful as this. The beach is bright with the light of other fires. Every fire pit has its own group of people laughing or dancing or just warming themselves. I press my toes hard into the damp sand. For some reason, I want to leave a mark.

We're halfway back when an enormous plane passes overhead. Air France. We both stop walking to stare up at it. The engine temporarily blots out all other sound.

"Paris would be nice," I say after it's gone.

"Pretty happy right where I am," he says.

I don't know when he stopped looking up at the sky and started looking at me instead.

"So you think Fifi's right? We're gonna dance better now we've gotten to know each other a little?" he asks.

"I think so," I say. The truth is I forgot that was the reason we started hanging out in the first place.

He stops walking. "One way to know for sure," he says. He

takes my right hand with his left and rests his other hand on my waist. We're almost in closed position. All I have to do is move my left hand and rest it on his shoulder, so I do.

"You want to practice right now?" he asks.

He slides his arm up from my waist to just under my shoulder blade. He uses the heel of his hand against my back to nudge me closer. Fifi would be proud of his lead technique. We are in perfect closed position.

There's at least six inches of space between us.

I can't quite get myself to look up at him, so I look at his clavicle instead.

"I really want to kiss you," he says.

Now I have to look up at him. "There's no kissing in dancing," I say.

He smiles a smile that's somehow wider than his face. He doesn't take his eyes off my lips. "Is that a yes?"

My heart slows all the way down. Strangely, I feel relieved. I know I'm going to kiss him. Honestly, nothing could stop me from kissing him. I've wanted to kiss him for a while now. Probably since our LaLaLand tour. Probably since before that.

The only reason I haven't yet is that I'm afraid. Because of my dad and the divorce. Because of the visions. What if I see our future? What if it's not a good one?

But I don't want to be afraid anymore.

I lean in and tilt my face up.

Our teeth collide.

He smiles against my lips and pulls away for a second to adjust our position. But then he puts his hands on either side of my face and kisses me again. I wrap my arms around his neck, wanting to get closer—*needing* to get closer. His hands slide down my back and then . . . lower. Never again will I make fun of his enormous hands. They are the perfect size.

"Wow, that was better than I thought it was gonna be, and I thought it was gonna be good," he says when we finally pull apart.

I laugh. "How much thinking about this have you been doing?"

"A fair amount," he says, and kisses me again, and it's more than good.

It's excellent.

Stupendous.

Phenomenal.

Prodigious.

Every synonym for *excellent* ever conceived.

I'll almost certainly worry about this kiss and what it means tomorrow, but for right now I lean in and kiss him again, happy to be in the here and now.

CHAPTER 25

The Ones You Don't See Coming, Part 1

"WHY DO YOU keep touching your lips like that?" Sophie asks. She imitates me by pressing two fingers against her lips.

Cassidy stops chewing her PB & J. "You *are* acting stranger than normal."

"Did something happen with you and X last night?" asks Sophie.

Across the table, Martin just watches me.

One of the hazards of having friends, especially longtime ones, is just how well they know you.

"We *might* have kissed," I say.

"See, I knew it!" Cassidy says, nudging Sophie's shoulder. "Didn't I say she had poufy just-kissed lips last night?"

"You did say that," Sophie says, laughing.

Martin joins in on the teasing. "Was it a good kiss?"

"Infinity on a scale of one to ten," I say, with a huge smile I can't seem to make smaller.

They tease me some more, with Cassidy claiming that she has kiss radar—"kissdar," she calls it. Sophie asks when we can have another bonfire with my "boyfriend."

Hearing her say *boyfriend* sends me into a small panic. First,

X and I are not officially together. Second, don't I know from the visions that things fall apart? Third, I don't know why I didn't see a vision of us last night. Maybe one of the rules of the visions is I can't see my own future? Or maybe I have to actually *see* the kiss for it to happen? That's fine with me. I like kissing with my eyes closed.

I stand up and grab my tray. "I'm going to get more chocolate milk. When I get back we can totally talk about something other than my lips."

I make my way over to the drinks counter, dodging squealing hugs, back slaps and high fives. The cafeteria is always loudest and most crowded on the first day back from a break, and that's definitely true today. But it's more than that. With only ten weeks to go until graduation, the seniors are especially sentimental. Never have there been so many breakups, make-ups, temporary hookups, declarations of devotion and general shenanigans. The hallways are a minefield of nostalgia bombs and regret grenades. Most conversations begin with either *Do you remember the time?* or *I wish I had.* Lots of group selfies are being taken. Kids are laughing louder and longer, as if whatever was just said is the funniest thing they've ever heard. Groups of friends who haven't hung out since freshman year are suddenly sitting together again. It's like everyone has realized that high school is ending, and they're trying to make every memory count.

I grab the last chocolate milk and head back to our table. When I get there, Sophie and Cassidy are gone.

"Where'd they go?" I ask Martin.

He shrugs. "No idea. Sophie had something to do and Cassidy went with her."

He waits for me to settle back into my seat before he starts his interrogation. "So I'm guessing you didn't have a vision after you kissed?"

I bounce a little in my seat. "Nope, not even a blip."

"Huh," he says. "I wonder why."

"I'm trying not to wonder why," I tell him.

"I'm happy for you, Eves. You guys are good together." He smiles, but I can feel that something's on his mind.

"What's up with *you*?" I ask.

"I think Danica really likes her new guy," he says. "She posts about him a lot. What if I missed my chance?"

I don't know what to say. I'm torn between wanting to make him feel better and not wanting to encourage him about something that's never going to happen.

"I don't think you missed your chance," I say.

The four-minute-warning bell rings, and we gather our things and leave. Our next class is on the third floor. Martin pushes the stairwell door open but then stops walking so suddenly that I almost run into him. "Oh my god," he says.

At first I think Danica must be here somewhere, because she always stops Martin in his tracks. But then I follow his gaze. It's not Danica.

It's Sophie and Cassidy standing right there in the middle of the staircase.

They're kissing.

And I see.

CHAPTER 26

❀

Sophie and Cassidy

SOPHIE AND CASSIDY outside Cassidy's enormous house. It's late at night. Cassidy is struggling to fit her key into the front door.

"Let me help you," Sophie says. She tries to take the key away from Cassidy, but Cassidy doesn't let go. Instead, she tries to pull Sophie in closer.

Sophie resists.

Cassidy says: "You're so pretty. How come it took me so long to notice how pretty you are?"

Sophie's dark eyes are hopeful and careful. "How drunk are you?" she asks, kind of teasing, kind of not.

Cassidy shakes her head. "You're pretty when I'm sober too," she says.

This time when Cassidy pulls her in, Sophie doesn't resist.

Cassidy leading Sophie through the doors of the planetarium at Griffith Observatory. Except for a guard and a tour guide, no one else is there.

"How did you do this?" Sophie asks, excited and awed.

Cassidy shrugs. "Might as well use my parents' money for something good," she says.

This moment right now, them kissing in the stairwell like no one's watching.

A late-night pool party in someone's backyard. Christmas lights strung across the sky. Kids strewn across the lawn.

Cassidy stumbles, almost falls into the pool, almost pulls Sophie in with her.

"God, Cassidy, how much did you drink?" Sophie asks.

"Don't be like that, Sophie," Cassidy says. "Relax."

Sophie looks down into the pool. It's lit from inside, glows blue-green against the night. To Cassidy she says: "But I thought you liked me like this."

The four of us at Surf City Waffle. Martin's USA map is folded and tucked between the syrup bottles and the wall.

Sophie and Cassidy are next to each other but not touching.

Cassidy is looking out the window. Her face says she wants to be someplace—anyplace—else.

Sophie is looking at Cassidy. Her face says she wants the same thing.

Cassidy starts ripping pages out of her Road Trip USA guidebook.

She doesn't look at Sophie, or any of us, as she leaves.

CHAPTER 27

The Ones You Don't See Coming, Part 2

THE VISION ENDS, and I'm back in the stairwell.

Sophie and Cassidy aren't kissing anymore. Instead, they're waving at Martin and me with goofy, happy expressions on their faces.

Martin nudges my shoulder. "Shit," he says. "You *saw* them, didn't you?"

I'm too rattled to talk, so I just nod.

Sophie and Cassidy realize something's wrong. They start walking down the stairs toward us.

I can't stay here and pretend to be happy for them when I understand how much pain they're going to cause each other.

"I have to go," I say, and push my way out the door.

And it's strange, because I've seen so many visions that I know to expect all relationships to end. But the ending of our friendship is a heartbreak I didn't see coming.

CHAPTER 28

The Fall

I KNOW SOMETHING'S wrong as soon as I get home from school.

First of all, the sliding glass door that leads to our patio and the common courtyard is wide-open. Mom hardly ever opens those doors because she hates nature. Mostly she hates bugs, but bugs are a part of nature, so. Her back is facing the room and she's gripping the doorframe, like she needs to steady herself.

I frown over at Danica. She's on the couch holding her phone to her ear with one hand and tugging on the ends of her Afro with the other. "Okay, Daddy," she says, using her usual happy-happy-joy-joy Dad voice.

I don't have a voice like that for Dad anymore. If Danica knew the truth of why Mom and Dad got divorced, she wouldn't either.

I spin on my heels, trying to escape upstairs and avoid talking to him.

Mom halts my escape. "Evie, your father needs to speak with you."

I start to protest, but she looks so blindsided that I stop. "What's going on?" I ask.

"Your father will explain." Her Jamaican accent is so thick, she sounds like she just immigrated yesterday.

Danica holds her phone out to me.

I take the phone but don't hold it to my ear right away. It always takes me a few seconds before I can say anything to him. Inside me are two Evies: the one that used to love him and the one that still does but doesn't want to.

"Hi," I say, using my flattest voice.

"Hi, sweet pea." He has me on speakerphone. I hate speakerphone.

"I don't like it when you call me that," I say.

He sighs. I can picture exactly what he's doing: pinching the bridge of his nose with one hand and rubbing his palm across the back of his neck with the other. "I have some news," he says.

I don't say anything.

"I wanted to tell you in person, but—"

He stops talking. What he wants to say is that since I refuse to visit him, he can't tell me anything in person.

Mom has stepped completely out onto the patio now.

Danica's big, dark eyes are scouring my face.

"It's about Shirley," he says.

For a second I think he's going to say they've broken up. For a second, I see us all back together at our house having blueberry pancakes for breakfast.

But that's not what he says. "We're getting married."

There was a time when he would've used an obscure phrase like *plighting our troth* instead of *getting married*. He'd have made me geek out over the etymology with him, and I would've teased him about his word nerdiness even though I'm a word nerd too.

We were so close before the divorce. We have the same sense of humor: slightly quirky, slightly cynical. We have the same outlook on the world: halfway between amused and bemused.

It's still hard for me to believe how far apart we are now.

He sighs into my silence. "Sweet pea, say something," he says.

"Don't call me sweet pea," I say.

"I know you're having a hard time with everything . . . ," he says, sympathy in his voice.

His sympathy just makes me angry. If it wasn't for his duplicity, I wouldn't need his sympathy. "Don't act like you care, because we both know that—"

"Stop," he says. Speakerphone makes his voice echo back on itself.

I sit down on the bottom step of the staircase. Now I understand why Mom was unsteady before.

Danica's frowning and shaking her head at me in disapproval.

"I want you to come to the wedding," he says.

"No," I say. "I'm not going."

"Evie, let's talk about this. I really want you—"

"No," I say. "I'm not going and you can't make me."

He sucks in a long breath and I know he's gearing up to flood me with words to try to convince me.

"I have to go to the bathroom," I say.

"Evie, I—"

"Really have to pee," I insist. "Going now."

He gives up. "Okay," he says.

I hang up but don't move from where I am on the stairs.

Mom comes back into the house and slides the glass doors

closed. With them shut, it feels like we're in our own little bubble, cut off from the world.

"Okay, well," Mom says. "I suppose we should talk."

Before she can launch into whatever parent talk she's about to give us, I ask her: "When did he tell you?"

"We spoke about it last night, but he wanted to tell you himself." She looks at Danica and clasps her hands in her lap. "How are you feeling about the news, D?" she asks.

"I feel fine about it," she says.

"What about you, Evie?" she asks.

"You know how I feel," I say.

She nods at the glass door. "I know this can be a challenging time," she starts, sounding like she's reading from a parenting book. *How to Talk to Your Children About Divorce.*

Except I'm not a child anymore. I'm almost eighteen. The visions have taught me more about how love really works than I ever wanted, or expected, to know.

I interrupt the speech she's giving us. "Mom, please don't make me go to the wedding."

She squeezes the arms of the chair. "It's important to your father."

"What about what's important to me?"

Danica slaps at her thigh. "Why are you always so mad at Dad?" she demands. "He didn't do anything wrong. They fell out of love and got divorced. It happens all the time."

I press my lips closed tight for a moment so I don't say anything I shouldn't say.

"Mom, please don't make me go," I beg.

"I think you're going to regret this, but I'm not going to

131

make you go." She stands up and heads for the hall closet. "You're really willing to upset your father like this?"

We both know the answer to that question.

"Promise me you'll at least think about it," she says.

I don't know if I've ever been so relieved. "Okay," I say, but only to make her feel better. I'm definitely not going to think about it.

Mom slips on a sweater. "I'm going for a walk," she says.

Danica shakes her head at me but doesn't say anything. She goes upstairs, leaving me alone on the couch.

Mom's wrong that I'll regret not going. What I would regret is seeing Dad kiss Shirley and learning their fate. I'd regret pretending to be happy for him. I'd regret seeing how happy he is in his new life, knowing that he was once ours. And most of all, I'd regret being there to commemorate the official end of our family.

——

I spend the rest of the evening doing nothing but responding (and not responding) to text messages. Sophie texts to say she's sorry she didn't tell me about her and Cassidy earlier, but isn't it great that they're together? She seems really happy. Cassidy texts too. She doesn't apologize for keeping their relationship a secret, and she's just as thrilled as Sophie is. *Can u believe she's my gf now??????*

Probably because I ran away from them earlier, they both want to know if I'm happy for them. I tell them that I am, and I want to mean it. But all I can see is what their relationship does to our friendship.

X texts right as I'm getting into bed.

My stomach does a happy little boogie when his name pops up on my screen, but then the boogie turns into a slow, heavy shuffle. What am I even doing? Between Dad's announcement and seeing the vision of Sophie and Cassidy, I don't need any more reminders of why being with X is a bad idea.

X: Hey, just saying hey
X: Was your day good?

It takes me ten minutes to come up with something that answers his question without encouraging any follow-up questions.

Me: Yup. Getting into bed now though
Me: Have a good night
X: OK
X: Good night

I stay awake for a long time, thinking. People are always saying stuff like "Take a chance on love." "Love is worth the risk." Etc.

But the visions have taught me differently. Dad getting engaged to the woman he cheated on Mom with taught me differently. Yes, falling in love requires a leap of faith. But people only jump because they don't know what the ground looks like. They *believe* their landing will be soft. That the ground is covered in soft stuff—feathers, down pillows, fluffy baby blankets, the shaggiest shag carpeting. But I've seen the ground. It is covered in lethal spikes fashioned from the bones of other jumpers.

The fall is not at all survivable.

CHAPTER 29

The Ones You Don't See Coming, Part 3

THE NEXT DAY, I manage to avoid Sophie and Cassidy while also pretending not to avoid them. In the morning, I go to my locker ten minutes earlier than usual. At lunchtime, when they text me from the cafeteria, I tell them I'm catching up on homework in the library. After school, I say I have to run errands for Mom.

But they suspect something's wrong.

Later that evening, Mom knocks on my door. "Your girls are here," she says. "I didn't know they were coming over."

I didn't either.

When I get downstairs, Sophie and Cassidy are both eating lemon-blueberry cookies from Mom's latest recipe experiments. Sophie's even drinking a glass of milk. Mom hangs out with us for a few minutes, asking the usual parent questions: *How are your folks? How's senior year? Ready for college?* She's done with her questions and they're done with their cookies faster than I want them to be. Mom goes back to watching *Sugared Up!* on TV.

"Let's go up to your room," says Cassidy.

She starts in as soon as I close my door. "Why are you avoiding us?"

"I'm not," I say, without meeting her eyes. We both know I'm lying. I try again. "I'm just really—"

"Busy. Yeah, we heard," says Cassidy.

Sophie walks to my bed and sits down. "We were wondering if seeing us together is weird for you."

"Why would it be weird?"

Cassidy sighs an impatient sigh, but Sophie keeps going. "Because Cassidy and I are a couple now and it makes things different for the four of us."

"Martin's fine with it," Cassidy interjects.

Sophie gives Cassidy a *please be quiet* look.

Cassidy mimes zipping her lips.

"What's going on with you?" asks Sophie.

"I'm fine," I say.

"No, you're not," Cassidy says. She pushes herself off the door and sits down next to Sophie on my bed. "You're cynical and a pain in the—"

Even though she's right, I feel defensive, like I'm the focus of some kind of intervention. But I'm not the one who needs saving.

"I don't think you guys should date," I blurt out.

"See?" Cassidy says turning to Sophie. "I knew it!"

Sophie looks down at her hands. "But why?"

"I'm worried about what'll happen to our friendship when you guys break up," I say as gently as I can. But there's no way to say a thing like that gently.

Sophie folds her arms tight across her chest and taps her foot. "Who says we're going to break up?"

"I mean . . . most couples break up eventually, right?"

Weirdly, it's Cassidy who tries to save me from myself. "Eves, come on. We're in love. Just be happy for us."

"I'm sorry," I whisper, shaking my head. "I can't pretend to be happy about the end of our friendship."

It's funny how many different kinds of silences there are. This one is shocked and disappointed and final.

I could tell them about Dad getting engaged to Shirley. Cassidy would get angry on my behalf and Sophie would be sympathetic. They'd both forgive me for the awful things I just said, but I don't. I'm just trying to stop them from hurting each other. From hurting all of us.

They stand at the same time. I feel their eyes on me, but I stare down at my feet. I don't look up as I hear my bedroom door open or as I hear their footsteps heavy on the stairs or as I hear the slam of the front door.

I know our friendship was going to change anyway. We're all going to separate colleges in the fall. But I thought we still had the rest of the summer for our epic road trip, for things to be the way they've always been. Now it turns out we don't have any time left.

CHAPTER 30

Off the Cliff

WHEN I GET home from school the next day, Mom and Danica are at the kitchen table peering at Danica's laptop screen.

Mom says a quick hello before she goes back to typing something.

Danica sighs and takes the laptop away from her. "No, Mom, you have to say something interesting about yourself," she whines. "Don't make it about being a mother. Make it about *you.*"

I don't have to see Mom's face to know she's smiling her *look how much you don't know yet* smile. "Those are the same thing, D!"

"But being a mom is not sexy."

"I'll remind you that you said that in about twenty years," Mom says.

I can't believe Danica is trying to talk Mom into dating. First Sophie and Cassidy, then Dad getting engaged and now this?

When Martin texts me five minutes later to meet him at La Brea Tar Pits, I get on my bike right away. Anything to get me out of my own head.

La Brea Tar Pits is called La Brea Tar Pits because it's on La Brea Avenue and has quite a few . . . tar pits. The largest one, Lake Pit, is just off the main entrance. The tar is greenish-black, thick and always oozing. Occasionally a bubble of stinky air burps to the surface.

Lake Pit is my favorite of the pits because it has one of the most macabre sculptures I've ever seen. It's of three enormous woolly mammoths—two adults and a baby. One of the adults is trapped waist-deep in tar. The other adult and the baby mammoth are safe on land, but the baby is clearly trumpeting in distress. Its mouth is frozen wide-open in a scream. Its trunk is rigid and pointed straight at the trapped mammoth. The other adult mammoth looks resigned.

The thing about the sculpture is that it captures a moment in time. You can read it two ways. Either the mammoth in the pit is done for and we're seeing its last seconds on earth. Or we're actually seeing the start of a miraculous escape.

How I read it changes depending on my mood.

Today, I decide that the mammoth in the pit is doomed.

I leave the mammoth family to their never-ending tragedy and climb to the top of the main hill and sit down on the grass. It's three o'clock. At this time of day the park population is mostly families with young children. I watch the little kids run up the hill and roll down it over and over again. I watch their anxious parents watch them anxiously.

Ten minutes later, Martin comes ambling up the hill. He's wearing a khaki shirt with khaki shorts and khaki hat. There's a red handkerchief tied around his neck.

"You look like a park ranger," I say.

"Thanks," he says. He sits down and wipes his forehead. With the handkerchief.

Before I can make fun of his outfit some more, I notice a little boy staring at the mammoth sculpture. His mom is with him. I can't hear what they're saying, but it's obvious that the boy is upset and his mom is trying to comfort him.

"That thing is such a bummer of truth," I say.

"I guess I don't need to ask what kind of mood you're in," Martin says.

I shrug and then sigh.

"Sophie and Cassidy told me about the fight," he says.

"Yeah, I figured," I say. I rest my head on his shoulder and look out over the park.

"Tell me what you see," he says, putting *see* in air quotes.

"You want me to tell you how people end up?" I ask, and he nods.

I look around, trying to find a couple on the verge of kissing. I find one, a guy and a girl, picnicking next to a big sycamore tree. I point them out to Martin. Once their vision ends, I tell him the outcome: "Semester-abroad trip to Japan. She falls in love with a Japanese girl."

"Huh," he says.

I find another couple holding hands. Again, I point them out to Martin. I don't have to wait too long for the inevitable kiss. "He proposes to her and she turns him down. She doesn't love him enough."

Another couple on a blanket are already kissing. He moves to New York.

We spend the next hour like this. I see all the things I expect

139

to. A lot of sweet beginnings. A lot of bitter endings. Affairs, deaths, illnesses, disenchantment and boredom.

After a while I can't take any more, and stop us.

People have certain tells when they're about to kiss: a light hand on a shoulder, or a touch to a waist, or a subtle closing down of the distance between bodies. The only way to live with this curse is to avoid seeing kisses in the first place. I need to learn to look away in time.

"Maybe you could tell them about the visions and what's going to happen," Martin says. He's talking about Sophie and Cassidy, but I know he doesn't really mean it. He's just as confused and frustrated as I am. It would be cruel to tell them what's going to happen to them. I'd be taking away their happiness.

I shake my head. "They'd never believe me." Couples in love believe they'll always be in love. It's one of the ways you know you're in love in the first place.

"Can't you just pretend you don't know?"

"Martin, you didn't see what I saw. It's awful. They're going to make each other so sad. Also, the biggest problem isn't that *they* break up. The problem is that they're going to break us *all* up. The four of us are not going to be friends anymore. No more epic road trip. No more group chats. No college spring breaks. No more anything."

"Yeah, I get it," he says. He looks back out at the couples in the park. "Don't they all seem so happy?"

I know what he means. After every vision, I study each couple to see if I can catch a glimpse of what's to come for them, but I can't find any evidence. Right now, in the same park as the doomed mammoths, they're happy.

My phone buzzes. It's X. I show Martin the phone and he makes a swoony face at me. I jab him with my elbow.

X: Hey
Me: Hi
X: You busy?
Me: Not really
X: Want to go out?
Me: When?
X: now

I tilt the phone so Martin can read my screen. "You should go," he says.

"It's probably a bad idea." I gesture out to the park, to all the couples whose visions I just watched and explained.

"Eves," he says. "Don't you think it counts for something that they're happy now?"

I don't know.

Maybe?

My phone buzzes again.

X: Or we can go some other time

I show Martin my phone again. "You gave him infinity on a one-to-ten kissing scale. How's this even a question?" he asks. "Text him back."

Me: We can go now
Me: Now's good

X: Great

X: Where should we go? Your turn to choose

Me: Why's it my turn?

X: I chose the lalaland tour and my show

X: You only chose the bonfire

X: So . . . two dates to one . . . your turn

Me: Those weren't dates

Me: They were hangouts

Me: Because of Fifi

X: Ahh I see

What does he see? I wonder.

X: So want to "hang out" again in an hour?

X: Text me where you want to go and I'll meet you there

Me: Ok

"You've got it bad," Martin says.

"It's not a rash," I tell him.

I bike home, change and then head back out. My stomach does somersaults of increasing complexity as I ride to meet X. What am I even doing? I wonder. Two nights ago I told Dad I wouldn't come to his wedding. I compared falling in love to jumping off a cliff. And just last night I told Sophie and Cassidy that all relationships end.

Hypocrite, thy name is Evie.

I press my fingers to my lips and hope I'm wrong about just how deadly the fall is.

CHAPTER 31

Definitely a Date

"WE'RE PLAYING POOL?" X asks as he walks up to where I'm standing underneath the sign for Wilshire Billiards.

"You don't want to?" I wasn't sure where to choose for our first official hangout/date/whatever we're calling it. Now I'm nervous he won't like it.

He stops a couple of feet away from me. "No, I'm just surprised, is all," he says.

We stare at each other. It's awkward and weirdly thrilling at the same time. The last time we saw each other there was kissing, but since we haven't decided what the kissing meant, neither of us knows what to do with our hands. Or lips.

I wave at him. He waves back at me. From two feet away.

Finally, he starts laughing, and then I do too.

"I'm really happy to see you," he says.

"Me too," I say. I feel like we should hug or something, but neither of us makes a move to do it.

He holds the door open for me. "So, pool, huh?"

"Well, I figured you'd be good at it. What else is there to do in Lake Elizabeth?"

"Wow," he says with pretend outrage. "Big-city snob."

143

I grin at him. But it's true that I can't imagine living anywhere but a big, diverse city.

Once we're inside, I head straight for the check-in counter. Julio, the sixtyish manager, spots me right away. "Señorita Evie," he sings out. "Long time no see." He leans over the bar counter for a double-cheek kiss and then looks out over my shoulder. "But where is your papa?"

"No dad today," I say, tugging on my backpack straps. "Just me and my friend X."

He and X exchange "hey, mans" and shake hands.

Julio looks back and forth between us, like he's trying to figure out if we're friends or *friends*. I can't tell what he decides. "Careful with this one," he tells X. "She's a shark."

"I'm getting that feeling," X says, tapping my pool-cue case where it sticks out of my backpack.

"Table seventeen," Julio says. He hands me the tray of balls and chalk. Table seventeen is the one Dad and I used to play on. It's out of the way, in the back right corner next to the dartboards that no one ever uses.

But I don't need more Dad reminders right now. Since I told him I'm not going to his wedding, he's texted me three separate times. The first was a photo of a Taco Night banner hanging from a lamppost on Wilshire Ave. The next was a list of all the food trucks that are going to be there. The third was a picture of us at Taco Night two years ago. We're both biting into chicken chimichangas (a deep-fried burrito made with rice, cheese, beans, shredded chicken and joy). Our eyes are closed and we are blissed out. I suppose I could always go with Mom or Martin or any of my other friends, but I know I won't.

No one else is a connoisseur like Dad. No one else will appreciate all the different types of salsa and what makes one better than the other.

I ask Julio for one of the tables on the left-hand side near the pinball machines instead.

Wilshire Billiards is not one of those dark, dingy pool halls you always see in movies. It's a big, clean space with pristine tables, polished cues and dark-wood mounted racks. The main lights are kept low, but every table has its own overhead light. I've always liked the way it looks—large areas of cool dark splashed by pools of yellow light.

It's late afternoon on Wednesday, so most of the tables are empty, except for the few up front that the old-timers use. They're mostly grizzled, grumpy old white guys, but they're excellent pool players. A couple of them recognize me and nod hello.

We get to our table and I take my cue from my backpack. Nice pool cues come in two pieces. I feel X's eyes on me as I unzip my case and screw the pieces together.

"What?" I ask.

"Is Julio right about you being a pool shark?"

"I'm okay," I say, downplaying my skills.

"Nah, you're a shark," he says, laughing. He picks a cue from the rack. "All right, teach me your ways, big-city snob," he says.

So I do.

I show him how to make sure a cue is straight by laying it flat on the table and rolling it. If it doesn't wobble, then it's straight. I show him how to rack the balls and how to apply chalk to the stick and powder to the area just between your thumb and forefinger, where the cue slides. Finally, I explain the rules: One person sinks the solid balls (solids), except the eight ball, and the other person sinks the striped balls (stripes). Whoever sinks all their balls first has to sink the eight ball.

"Let me show you how to break." I line up to the table and hit the white cue ball into the rack. The balls scatter across the table.

I reset the rack for him. "Now your turn," I say.

He lines up to the table. And it's hard to imagine him doing more things wrong than he does. He holds the cue way too far up, rests it on the wrong two fingers and doesn't line his head up with the shot. When he breaks, his stick glances off the cue ball so it only travels a few inches before stopping.

He grins at me. "Maybe I should try that again," he says.

I laugh. "That was tragic." I shake my head. But secretly, I'm kind of thrilled to have an excuse to get closer to him and fix his form.

I think of every straight rom-com I've ever watched with a pool-hall scene. Usually going to play pool is the guy's suggestion, because:

1) he can show off his skills.

and

2) he can get up close and personal with the girl under the guise of showing her proper technique.

I reset the rack. "Here, let me show you," I say. I stand right next to him, lean over the table and demonstrate the proper hold.

He tries again. This time the cue ball does hit the rack, but with so little force the balls barely even move.

I slap my hand over my mouth to cover my laugh.

This time after I reset the rack, I scoot around the table, lean over and put my arm on top of his so I can adjust his hold.

He turns his head. Suddenly his face (and lips) are *just right there.*

"Thanks for helping me," he says.

"You're welcome," I say back.

His eyes drop to my lips and stay there.

"The sign outside says Wilshire *Billiards,* not Wilshire *Make Out,*" says a voice—Julio—from somewhere behind us.

I practically leap away from X. "I was just teaching him how to play."

X stays where he is, laughing down into his outstretched arm.

Julio smiles and shakes his head. "Call it what you want, but keep it PG-13 in here for me. I know your dad, for Jesus's sake," he says as he walks away.

X just laughs some more.

I poke him with my cue and tell him to be quiet.

"All right, let me see if I got this," he says, looking back down at the table. Suddenly, his body transforms itself. His stance goes from sloppy to perfect. He's holding the cue exactly right, and his head is lined up perfectly.

He breaks with a loud smack and sinks one solid. Then he proceeds to sink four more in a row before just missing the sixth. He turns around, catches my eye and gives me the cockiest grin I've ever seen.

"Guess you were right about there being nothing to do in Lake Elizabeth," he says.

I've. Been. Had.

I thump my cue on the ground. "Why'd you pretend you didn't know how to play?"

"Maybe I wanted you to teach me," he says with a wink. "Or maybe it's because you made fun of my hometown. Let's see what you got, city girl."

I narrow my eyes at him. "Oh, you're going down, country boy," I say. I shoot the nine but miss. I'm still flustered by his trickery and by how good he is. I don't get another shot to win, because he sinks his remaining solid and then the eight ball to win.

I swear louder than I should and he just laughs at me. "I like this side of you," he says.

"Don't try to distract me." I pretend-scowl at him, but I'm actually happy that he's as good as he is. Pool is a lot more fun when you have actual competition.

I win the next two games, but he wins the fourth and fifth. I take the sixth when he misses an easy bank for the eight ball. We're tied at three games all.

"Should we just leave it tied?" he asks.

"Why? Are you afraid to lose?"

"Yeah, don't say I didn't give you a chance to get out of this with your dignity," he says.

I roll my eyes. "You let me worry about my dignity," I say. "But can we eat something first? I'm starving, and their burgers are really good."

We order at the bar and then sit at one of the small tables up front.

X takes a look around. It's more crowded now than when we first got here. One of the old-timers is at the jukebox, no doubt putting on a country-western song from sometime in the last century. I look over at Julio, who laugh-shrugs at me. He's been promising to get better songs for the jukebox for years.

"So you and your dad used to come here?" X asks.

"Every Sunday morning. He and Julio would trade off giving me lessons, and then we'd just play for hours."

"Man, your dad sounds great," he says before remembering that I don't think he's so great. "Sorry, I forgot about—"

"No, it's okay," I say. "I mean, I used to think he was great too. Honestly, it's part of why this whole thing sucks so much. It's one thing that he cheated on Mom, but I feel like he betrayed my idea of him too. And now he's getting remarried and there's no going back to the way it was before. I dunno. I'm not making sense."

"Shit, Evie, I didn't realize he was getting married again." He puts his hand on top of mine for a few seconds. "I get what you're saying, though. It's like he's not who you thought he was."

"Yeah, like in the movies when there's a twist and it turns out the person you thought was the good guy is actually the villain." My heart feels tight in my chest. I don't want to make things so heavy between us, but I feel like I need to tell him the truth about how I'm feeling about the world.

"I wasn't always like this," I say.

"Like what?"

Julio comes by with the burgers right then, which is good, because it gives me some time to figure out what I'm trying to say.

149

X bites into his burger and then makes a happy, *that's so delicious* sound. We eat for a little while before he prompts me again: "You weren't always like what?"

I lean forward. "I don't know if I believe in this stuff anymore."

"What stuff?" he asks, chewing slowly.

I wave my hand between us. "Dating."

He puts down his burger and his eyes are steady on me as he waits for me to go on. "Remember at the bonfire you asked me if Sophie and Cassidy ever dated?" I ask.

"Yeah, why?" I see the moment he figures it out. "They hook up or something?"

I nod.

His eyes roam over my face. "How come you're sad about it?"

I don't want to tell him about our fight and how I haven't seen them all week. "I don't think they're right together, and when they break up it's going to ruin our friendship."

"Who says they're gonna break up?"

How do I explain this to him without telling him about the visions?

"Nothing lasts," I say. "My parents used to be so happy. If you'd met the Evie from a year and a half ago and told her that her dad would cheat on her mom and they'd get divorced and her dad would be getting remarried, she would've made merciless fun of you."

"Well, I don't know what the old Evie was like, but I like the new one a lot," he says. "It's okay you're feeling cynical these days. It's okay if you don't trust the world so much right now. You have good reasons."

150

And just like that, I like him even more than I already did. He's so surprising, this boy, swagger and insight and gentleness all mixed up together.

We finish our burgers and head back to our pool table. "Ready to lose?" he asks, picking up his cue.

I don't even bother to narrow my eyes at him. As soon as he's done racking, I break, sinking two solids. After that, I proceed to run the table like it's my job. Only the eight ball is left. I turn and give him the cockiest grin I know how to.

"I deserve that," he says as he busts out laughing.

"Maybe I'll sink it with my eyes closed," I say.

"No way," he says. "No way you're gonna take that kind of chance."

But it's an easy shot for me. I'm not taking much of a chance at all. I sink it with my eyes closed. When I open my eyes again, he's right there next to me.

He takes my cue from me and lays it on the table. "Nice game," he says, pulling me into his arms for a hug.

I wrap my arms around his waist and press my face against his chest.

We stay that way for a little while, until he says, "We can go slow if you want." He pulls back a little to look down at my face. "I mean, assuming you want to do this again. With me."

It's sweet how nervous he is. I smile up at him. "Okay, let's go slow."

"Does this mean we can officially call this a date?" he asks.

I laugh and put my head back on his chest. "It's definitely a date," I say.

CHAPTER 32

Let's Taco 'Bout It

MOM HAS HER very first app date tonight. His name is Bob. He's a pediatrician. An oncological pediatrician. When I asked her why she thought a handsome doctor had never been married at age forty-seven, she looked at me and said, "He saves the lives of children, Evie. Children with cancer."

I'm not supersure what one thing has to do with the other, but I let it go.

"Trust me, you look beautiful," Danica says to Mom as they come downstairs.

How Danica talked Mom into shimmery gold eyeshadow and red lipstick, I don't know. But she's right. Mom looks gorgeous. She's wearing a dark-blue midlength dress that flares at the hips with her favorite pair of practical-but-still-sexy heels. The last time I saw her wear those shoes was out to dinner with Dad.

She checks her face in the vestibule mirror and turns to Danica. "You sure about this lipstick? You don't think it's too—"

"Come hither?" I fill in for her. Fire engines are less red.

"Yes, that," Mom says.

Danica waggles her eyebrows. "Getting him to *come hither* is the point."

"Ha!" says Mom. She checks herself in the mirror again, trying out different smiles. I'm happy she's excited and stressed that she's excited.

The doorbell rings.

"Is that him?" I ask, getting up from the couch. "Shouldn't you meet him at the restaurant so he doesn't know where we live in case he turns out to be a serial killer cancer doctor?"

"I *am* meeting him at the restaurant," Mom says, frowning at the door.

Danica looks through the peephole. "Oh, it's Dad," she says, voice bright and happy. She throws the door open.

From the look on Mom's face, I can tell she's just as surprised as I am.

Mom walks to the door. "I didn't know you were coming over this evening." Her voice is hard, harder than I expect, like she's scolding him.

Dad hears it too and wipes his palm across his mouth. "Grace," he says. "You look nice."

At the compliment, Mom takes a step back. She folds her arms across her chest and waits. "What's this about?"

"Sorry about this," he says. "I was trying to surprise Evie."

"Safe to say you've surprised us all," says Mom. Her Jamaican accent is slight, but it's there. She steps aside and lets him in.

I haven't seen him in six months, not since the night he took Danica out to dinner to meet Shirley and I refused to go.

He looks the same, and he looks not the same. Like, I've never seen him in that green shirt before. And his Afro has

153

some gray in it. Even his mustache has some gray in it. And is he thinner? I don't know. It might be one of those things where you only notice the changes in someone after you've been away from them for a while. Probably he was gray before he left us. But the green shirt is new. New to me, at least.

"Evie," he says. "It's Taco Night." He says it like it's sacred. Like we're in church and a corn tortilla taco is the sacrament. Which, okay, yes. Taco Night is a religious experience and missing it is definitely a sacrilege. But it's his fault we're missing it.

He reaches into the pocket of his blazer (new) and takes out his glasses (also new).

"Look," he says. "I got us Front of the Line tickets for Mariscos Chente."

I stand there, mute. All six of their eyeballs eyeball me. Dad's are hopeful. Danica's are watchful. And Mom's are . . . hard to read. No one has a better poker face than her. It's part of being a nurse, I think.

Mom takes my hand. "Let's go upstairs and talk."

She closes the door once we're in her bedroom. "I want you to go with your father."

A thing I never noticed before: she only refers to him as "your father" these days instead of "your dad."

"Mom, I don't want to—" I start to protest.

She talks over me. "You're already not going to his wedding."

"You know why I'm not going," I say.

"We're not talking about that." Her voice is firm. She meets my eyes and holds them steady. "You know what one of the hardest parts of being a mom is?"

"What?"

"Watching your child do something you know they'll regret."

And that does it. I agree to go. I don't want anything to be harder for her, especially when it comes to Dad.

I get back downstairs in time to hear Danica telling Dad about her new boyfriend. "His name is Archer," she says.

"Archer is a profession, not a name," he says, in typical Dad fashion.

Before I can stop myself, I'm playing along. "It's more of an Olympic sport than a profession, really."

"Summer or winter?" Dad asks.

"Summer, for sure."

Dad and I smile at each other until I remember I'm not supposed to smile at him anymore. It would be so easy to slip back into this rhythm with him.

Danica rolls her eyes in our general direction. "Anyway, Archer is his name, and he's great."

I walk to the door, ready to leave. Danica and Dad hug and say goodbye. Mom and Dad just nod at each other. And we're off.

———

It's only a fifteen-minute walk from our apartment complex to where we're going. Here's how we spend the first five minutes:

Dad: How's school?
Me: Fine.

Long, awkward silence.

Dad: I heard from Danica that you're ballroom dancing. How's that going?
Me: Fine.

Longer, more awkward silence.

Dad: How are your friends?
Me: I think you can guess the answer to this one, right?

He stops walking.

I stop too. "It's not like you can bribe me into forgiving you with tacos, anyway," I say.

He throws his hands up. "What can I bribe you with, then?"

I fold my arms tight across my chest and stare down at my shoes. Decaying jacaranda leaves, more brown than purple, litter the sidewalk. It's funny how they're so beautiful on the tree and such a nuisance off of it.

"Can we call a taco truce for the night?" he asks.

The last time I heard him sound like this was when he promised me and Danica that he didn't love us any less just because we wouldn't be living together anymore.

I sigh and agree to the truce with a nod.

He smiles like I've told him he's best dad in the world or something.

I really miss thinking that he was the best dad in the world.

We start walking again. "Should we devise a conquering strategy?" he asks. At my confused look, he goes on: "We need to decide which trucks to partake of and in what order."

I can't help smiling. "You mean because of the great chimichanga incident of yesteryear?"

"Those who don't learn from history—"

"Are doomed to repeat it," I finish for him, with pretend seriousness.

Last time we started with the fried meats, which was a mistake. Too heavy. By three chimichangas in, we were full.

"Let's start with the ceviches," he says.

We agree and spend a few more minutes deciding which trucks to hit and when. Once that's settled, we move on to talking about our favorite sport, the National Spelling Bee. I used to argue that it wasn't a sport, but then Dad convinced me it is. "Have you seen how much those kids sweat while they're thinking?" he asked.

We talk about last year's winning word—*prospicience*—which, weirdly enough, given my current predicament, means "foresight."

We don't talk about how we missed watching it together.

We don't talk about how this year's competition is only two months away and how we probably won't watch that together either. Maybe he doesn't watch it at all anymore. I wonder if Shirley is a word geek.

We cross Sixth Street and cut through Pan Pacific Park until we're finally on Wilshire Boulevard. Taco trucks gleam in the distance.

"I smell my future," Dad says.

"It smells like salsa," I say back.

He laughs and I laugh too.

We eat until our stomachs hurt. It turns out it doesn't matter if you start with the lighter foods if you still eat too much of them.

On our way back, he tells me terrible Mexican food jokes:

Q: What do you call a nosy pepper?

A: Jalapeño business.

and

The first tortilla asks the second tortilla: "Do you want to taco 'bout it?"

The second tortilla says: "No. It's nacho problem."

They're such bad jokes that I can't help laughing. I think the phrase *dad joke* was invented because of *my* dad.

We move on from bad jokes to talking about our favorites from the evening. Tacos al pastor for him. Shrimp ceviche for me. It feels like every other Taco Night, except we're both going home to someplace new.

We're just a couple of apartment buildings away from home when he says he has something to tell me.

"Shirley and I are thinking about postponing the wedding," he says.

Hope flashes in the small, stubborn place in my heart, the part that used to read too many romance novels. Maybe this means he's reconsidering. Maybe this means there's hope for him and Mom. But the feeling only lasts for a second. I know that's not what he means.

"Why?" I ask.

"To give you more time to get used to the idea. I want you to be there. It's important to me."

The earnestness on his face is hard to look at. I want to say yes. No. I want to want to say yes. But I can't pretend to be happy for him and Shirley.

Still, it's nice that he wants me to come.

I shake my head. "Dad, don't," I say. "Don't postpone for me."

I can see he wants to force the issue, to pull dad rank, but he doesn't.

"Okay," he says. "Promise me you'll think about it."

It's not lost on me that both he and Mom have asked me to make this promise.

Before I can answer him, someone calls out to me. "Hey, Evie."

It's X. My heart does this weird interpretive dance thing in my chest. His dreads are down and his eyes are bright black and focused on me. His guitar is strapped across his back.

Dad steps closer, like he might need to protect me from X's good looks.

"Hey, X," I say, and do a little wave.

Dad clears his throat.

Right. Introductions. "Dad," I say, "this is X. X, this is my dad."

Dad guffaws. "Your name is X? Like the unknown variable *x*?"

"Your daughter already let me have it about my name, Mr. Thomas," X says, holding out his hand for a shake.

"I should hope so," says Dad. He points at X's hair. "Are those dreads religious or just fashionable?"

"Purely for fashion, Mr. T."

"Go the distance with my name, son. It's Mr. Thomas," Dad says. "What about the guitar? That only for fashion too?"

X laughs. "No sir, Mr. Thomas. The guitar is real."

Dad proceeds to quiz X on his past and future history. X conveniently leaves out the dropping-out-of-high-school part.

I guess Dad is satisfied with X's answers, because eventually he says: "Am I okay to leave you two alone together?"

"Yes, of course," I say.

Dad turns to me. "One more joke before I go," he says.

"All right," I say, already shaking my head in anticipation of how awful it will be.

"Have you heard the one about the quesadilla?" he asks.

I play along. "Why, no, I haven't heard it."

He waves me off dramatically. "Never mind, it's too cheesy."

X laughs with his fist over his mouth. "Good one, Mr. Thomas."

Pleased as punch is an expression Dad uses often. Right now he is. "I like you, despite the ridiculous name," he says to X.

"Thanks, Mr. T," X says. Then, "I'm just messing with you, sir," to Dad's glare.

"Please think about what I said about the wedding," Dad says to me.

"Okay," I say, and I really mean it. Probably tomorrow I'll be angry again, but right now my tummy is full of delicious food and my face is still smiling at his bad jokes and he feels just like he used to feel, like my very first best friend forever. He pulls me in for a hug and squeezes me tight and I squeeze him right back, wishing in that same small stubborn place that this feeling would last forever.

CHAPTER 33

The Time We Get

X AND I stand on the sidewalk and watch Dad drive away. Once his car disappears around a bend, I turn to X.

"Aren't you guys supposed to be rehearsing tonight?" I ask.

"We did, but we stopped early." He tugs on his guitar strap. There's something sad in his voice that makes me look at him more closely, but he doesn't say anything else about why they stopped. "We finished up the music for 'Black Box.' Thought I'd come by and surprise you with it. That okay?"

I nod. I know we're supposed to be taking it slow, but it's more than okay with me that he spontaneously showed up at my door.

Once he's inside, I offer him some water, which he drinks down in one gulp. I give him another, and he gulps that one too. The third one he just sips. We leave the kitchen and hover in the area between the dining and living rooms. He unstraps his guitar and leans it against the wall next to the sliding glass doors.

"So you and your dad went out?"

I explain to him about our Taco Night tradition, and how Dad surprised me.

"How was it?" he asks.

"It was . . . nice, actually," I say.

"Kind of pissed you had a good time, right?"

"How'd you know that?"

"For a while after Clay died, I used to get mad at myself for having fun playing music without him."

"When did you stop?"

"Haven't yet," he says.

I ask him if he wants a tour of the apartment, before realizing that a tour will include my room. Does showing him my bedroom count as taking it slow? It does not.

He follows me upstairs. I point out our lone bathroom and both Mom's and Danica's rooms.

"When do I get to meet your sister?" he asks.

"She has a boyfriend," I blurt out, answering a question he didn't ask. Why did I do that?

He watches me for a second. "And I can't meet her because he keeps her locked up in a fairy-tale tower?" The small smile at the corner of his lips says he's teasing me.

"No, I just mean she's out tonight. With her boyfriend. So you can't meet her."

He nods, but his smile stays where it is. "Your mom?"

"Also on a date. And this is my room," I say when we get to the end of the hallway. The door is closed. I stop a couple of feet away and stare at it.

He looks back and forth between the door and me. "You going to open it with your mind, or . . . ?"

"What? No. Telekinesis isn't my superpower. I was just thinking about something else."

163

"Okay," he says. We go back to door-staring.

"Lemme just check there's nothing weird in there," I say. I open the door just enough to squeeze my body through and then close it in his face.

By "nothing weird," I mean no errant underwear or anything else embarrassing. I shove two bras into my chest of drawers.

I make my bed.

Finally, I open the door. "Come on in," I say, trying for blasé, but it's hard to be blasé when you've just been hiding your underwear.

He stops inside the threshold and does a slow perusal of my room. He starts on the left with my closet, travels past that to my desk under the window, then to my bookshelf and chest of drawers before winding up on my bed.

I feel (metaphorically) naked.

He heads for my bookshelf. I can't blame him. It's what I would do too. He scans my books, and I try to guess what he's learning about me.

"You label your shelves," he says, turning to look at me.

"Is that good or bad?"

"Not sure yet," he says with a laugh. "What happened to all these books, though?" he asks, waving his hand over the Contemporary Romance section.

"Just not into them anymore."

He nods like he understands, because he does understand. He knows what it's like to have a "before" and "after" period in your life. There's a pre-divorce Evie and a post-divorce Evie. They look the same but aren't.

He touches the empty shelf. "Did you have a favorite?"

I don't even have to think about it. *"Cupcakes and Kisses,"* I say. The scene with the two chefs making out while making dessert flashes in my head. I decide it's time to leave my bedroom. X is starting to look edible.

"Okay, well, that's my room," I say. "There's nothing else to see here. Why don't we go back downstairs now?" That sounded much more casual in my head.

"Yes, indeed, shall we?" he says, mock-formal, totally making fun of me.

We go downstairs and he grabs his guitar before we head out to the patio.

It's late, almost nine. Lights are on in most of the other apartments. Everyone's patios are splashed with little pools of orange-yellow light. Someone, probably Mrs. Chabra, is cooking. The night air smells delicious, like turmeric and onions.

We both sit, me in the armchair and him across from me on the sofa. He gives me a small smile and stares off into the courtyard.

Something's definitely bothering him. "Are you okay?" I ask.

He covers his eyes with his hands. "It's the anniversary of when Clay . . . I mean, it was a year ago today. I didn't think it would be so hard. Tonight at practice we were all trying to act like everything was normal." He stares up at the sky for a few seconds.

"Want to talk about it?" I say after a little while.

At first, I'm not sure he's going to answer. He strums his

guitar, changes chords a couple of times and strums some more.

"The thing that gets me is how stupid it was. He was crossing the street. Some guy was driving and sending a text. It's just so fucking preventable. It's the law. Don't text and drive."

He strums just once, loud and angry. "And it wasn't a kid. Not one of us irresponsible teenagers. It was a fucking adult. Who was supposed to know better. Isn't that the one good thing about being a grown-up? You know better?" He scoffs. "They don't know shit. They're just better at pretending."

He strums again, but quieter this time. "We had a show. End-of-summer concert series at Barrington Park. He was late, but he was always late, so I didn't know—" He shakes his head, like he did something wrong by not knowing. "His sister called. She's the one who told us what happened. By the time me and Jamal and Kevin got there, he was already gone. He died in the street."

He leans forward, hunches over the guitar so it looks like he's cradling it. His locs waterfall his face, so I can't see if he's crying or not. I don't know what to do or what to say to help him, but I have to help him.

I stand up and take the guitar from his hands and put it off to the side.

Without it, he slumps over even farther and covers his face with his hands. I sit down next to him and put my arm around his shoulder. He leans into me and I wrap my other arm around him.

I don't tell him everything is all right, because it's not. His best friend died a stupid, completely avoidable death, and it sucks, and it doesn't make sense, and everything isn't all right.

I don't know how much time passes, but after a while, he straightens up. I let him go. He wipes his eyes with the heels of his hands and gives a smile somewhere between embarrassment and gratitude.

"I'll get you some water," I say, not because I think he needs more to drink, but to give him time to pull himself together. It's what I'd want.

"Nah, I'm good," he says.

"I'm trying to give you a minute alone," I tell him.

His eyes are damp and red around the rims. "I get what you're doing, Evie," he says. "And I appreciate it, but I'd like it if you stayed with me. If that's okay."

I don't know how he manages to let himself be so vulnerable. I sit back down next to him, and we watch the sky get darker together.

I ask him to tell me about Clay and he does. They met in a music store when they were kids. Both of them were just starting guitar lessons, and their dads had taken them to the store to get sheet music.

"He was in the guitar section holding a bass that was about fifteen sizes too big for him. We were friends as soon as I sat down next to him."

He looks at me. "He would've liked you. Would've liked how snarky you are."

"I've never been snarky a day in my life."

He laughs. "Says the snarky girl snarkily."

Across the way, Mrs. Chabra starts playing music. The song starts off slow but gets faster almost immediately.

He taps his feet to the rhythm. "You ever dance to Bollywood music?" he asks.

I shake my head.

"One of my buddies back home is Indian American. Man, his parents know how to throw a party. The music is loud and the dancing is wild." He's grinning now, and I've never been happier for Mrs. Chabra's music. "None of this closed-position ballroom stuff," he says.

"Show me," I say.

He springs up and suddenly he's all movement—neck popping, wrists twisting, hips circling. He even does some knee slapping. He looks like an enthusiastically malfunctioning robot.

I'm sure he's not doing any Indian dance any actual justice, but it's so nice to see him smiling instead of crying that I forgive him.

I join him, dancing the moves I've "learned" from the handful of Bollywood movies I've seen. Pretty soon we're trying to one-up each other with more and more elaborate neck and wrist action. Somehow my dance morphs into the Robot. He stops dancing to laugh at me and I (robotically) flip him off. He laughs even more, and then he's looking at me the same way he did on the beach right before we kissed. His hands are on my waist and my palms are flat against his chest.

A light flashes in my periphery. I know I should pay attention to it, but all my concentration is on precisely how close X's lips are to mine.

X is the one that stops us. "I think someone's home," he says.

I step back just in time for Mom to turn the corner into the living room.

She slides the patio door open. "What exactly is happening out here?" she asks.

We aren't doing any of the things parents worry about—sex, drugs, experimental body piercings—but I still feel caught.

Mom scrutinizes my state of dress. Once she's satisfied I'm wearing all my clothes, and in the way they're supposed to be worn, she downgrades her face from scowl to frown. "Who's this?" she asks.

"This is X," I say.

"Nice to meet you, Ms. Thomas."

"Oh yes. You're the dancing boy. The grandson," she says. "How's the practicing coming along?"

"Good, good. Our instructor hasn't killed us yet," X says.

"Funnily enough, I didn't realize I was in danger of losing my firstborn," Mom says, deadpan.

X laughs. "Ballroom is deadlier than most people realize, Ms. Thomas."

Mom tilts her head to the side, considering. "You're funny," she says. "Well, it's nice to meet you. Hopefully both you and my daughter will survive the dancing."

She's halfway inside when it occurs to me why she's in such a good mood. "Mom, how was your date?"

"It was . . . really good," she says with a happy little smile. "We're seeing each other again next weekend. We're going hiking."

"But you hate nature," I remind her. "And you don't hike."

"I do now," she says back with another smile. "Your curfew is in five minutes."

X turns to me once the sliding glass door is all the way closed. "Man, that was close," he says. "Can't have your mom's first impression of me be bad. I need for her to like me."

"She likes you," I say, so earnestly I'm sure he knows I'm talking about myself. "My dad likes you too."

"That's good," he says.

We stare at each other for another few seconds. If only Mom had come home a minute later.

"Well, I guess I should get going," he says. He picks up his guitar and straps it across his back. "I didn't get to play the song for you."

"Next time," I say. I walk him back through the apartment and out the front door.

"Think your friends would be up for a bonfire tomorrow night?" he asks.

I almost agree before I remember the state of things with Sophie and Cassidy.

"That's not such a good idea," I say.

He rubs the back of his neck. "Sorry, I know you said you wanted to go slow."

"No, no, it's not that," I say, rushing to reassure him. I tell him what happened with Sophie and Cassidy.

When I get to the end, he tilts his head at me, confused. "Wait. You broke up with them because they started dating each other?"

"Not because they *started*. Because they'll eventually *stop* dating. They're going to break each other's hearts. It's too painful to watch."

"So you're not friends with them?"

"We're friends. We just don't hang out anymore." I know how nonsensical this sounds. I try for a smile to lighten the mood and move us on from here, but it doesn't work.

"Evie, you ditched the friends you've had since middle school."

I let out a frustrated sigh. "I can't explain."

"Because it doesn't make sense. Even if your guess is right and they break up and screw everything up, look at all the time you're missing with them *right now.*" He turns and stares down the street like there's something out there he's been hoping to see. "People don't come back, Evie. The time we get is the time we get." His voice is urgent, like he really needs me to understand the thing he's trying to tell me. He'd give anything to have another day with Clay.

I take a step down and wrap my arms around his waist. It takes him a few seconds before he puts his arms around me too.

"I'll think about what you said," I say.

"Was this our first argument?" he asks.

"I think so."

"Wasn't too bad," he says, grinning down at me.

I smile back up at him. "We can try harder next time."

CHAPTER 34

I Got You, Babe

I WAKE UP knowing what I have to do. It's Sunday, which means it's Surf City Waffle brunch day. When I text Martin to tell him I'm going to meet them there, he says to go to Cassidy's house instead. Sophie didn't want to go to SCW if we weren't all going to be together. I get on my bike and try not to think about all the togethers we're going to miss in the future. X's words from last night come back to me. *The time we get is the time we get.*

The first time I ever visited Cassidy's house in Beverly Hills, I was in middle school. Her house is so big I remember thinking that Dad had gotten the address wrong and taken me to a hotel or country club. But no.

I ring the bell and Martin answers the door. Instead of hello, he says, "Just warning you, they're still pretty mad."

"How mad is pretty mad?"

"Be prepared to offer up one of your organs," he says, and closes the door behind me.

"Who's angrier?"

"Sophie's less likely to take a swing at you."

"Okay," I say.

"Also, you should know that they really believe in public displays of affection. They kiss all the time. They call each other 'babe' all the time."

"Even Cassidy?"

"Especially Cassidy. You don't know the things I've seen, Eves," he says.

I shudder-laugh. More shudder than laugh. Sixty-three percent shudder.

"Thank God you're back," he says. "It's not the same without you."

He leads me through the house and out to the pool.

At first, they don't see me. They're too busy canoodling in the water. I don't want to interrupt, so I take a seat at the outdoor dining table. It's spread with fancy plates, actual silver silverware and champagne glasses. I see the remnants of waffles and a few different syrups.

"Did you guys get takeout from SCW?" I ask.

"No, it turns out they have a family chef now," Martin says.

"Jesus, they're so rich," I say.

"Yup," he says, and offers me a plate.

I'm too nervous to eat, so I just sit there and wait. I don't have to wait long for Cassidy to realize I'm here. "I don't remember inviting you over," she says, using her *I'm about to set something on fire* voice.

Martin mimes pulling out and offering an organ.

I start with the basics instead. "Hey, guys."

Sophie gets out of the water, wraps herself in a towel and

sits down on a lounge chair. "Hi, Evie," she mumbles, but she doesn't look at me.

Cassidy gets out of the pool and follows Sophie to the lounge. She ignores me completely. To Martin she says: "Why is she here?"

"I came to apologize," I say.

In her eyes, I can see Sophie wants to forgive me. She rests her hand on Cassidy's shoulder and squeezes, but Cassidy just folds her arms tight.

I look to Martin for help. "Grovel," he mouths.

I didn't think it was going to be this hard to get back to being friends. But now I'm realizing that it might not be up to me. What if they decide not to forgive me? Then X will have been right: *I'll* be responsible for our breakup. Not them.

"Why'd you say we should break up?" Cassidy asks. "It's me, right? You think I'm not good enough for Sophie?"

I can't believe she thinks that. Or, I can believe it. It's basically what her parents have been telling her all her life with their constant neglect.

I walk over to the lounge chair and squat in front of her. "No, Cassidy. It's not that at all. It's just me. Ever since Mom and Dad—"

Sophie squeezes Cassidy's shoulder again. "See, I told you," she says.

I'm happy to know that Sophie's been holding on to her faith in me.

But Cassidy isn't ready to forgive me yet. "Jesus, just get over it already. Ever since it happened, you've been—"

Sophie interrupts her. "What Cassidy means is we miss the

174

old Evie. Not everyone's going to end up like your parents. Some people are happy."

"I'm sorry I've been so selfish. I've been a complete idiot," I say to Cassidy.

She shakes her head, but I catch a glimpse of a small smile. "Complete idiot bitch," she says.

"I'm sorry I was a complete idiot bitch," I say, smiling back at her. "I didn't mean any of what I said. I'm so happy you guys are happy."

Cassidy beams. It might be the first known beaming in Cassidy history.

"You're beaming."

She scowls. "I don't beam."

"Yes you do," says Sophie.

And then Cassidy does another un-Cassidy-like thing: she blushes.

We all stare at her.

"Fuck," she says.

We spend the rest of the day catching up. Martin's right that Sophie and Cassidy are charter members of the public displays of affection fan club. And the word *babe* needs to be exorcised from their vocabulary. And it really is strange watching them touch and kiss.

But I can't deny that they're happy. Really happy.

I wish I could make it last for them. That's the superpower I *should* have, making love last forever.

We keep hanging out until it's time for me to head home for dinner.

Sophie pulls me into a hug. "We missed you, Evie."

Cassidy joins the hug. "Next time we won't forgive you so easily."

"This was easy?"

"You still have all your organs," Martin says, wrapping his arms around all of us.

"That's true," I say. "I missed you guys too."

CHAPTER 35

Bachata Monday

"I'M GLAD YOU made up with them," X says as soon as he walks into the studio on Monday evening.

I texted him last night to tell him I fixed things with Sophie and Cassidy.

"Me too," I say. "You were right."

He pulls me into a hug. "I'm right a lot. You're going to have to get used to that."

"Oh, shush," I say. Our eyes connect. The air between us shifts from teasing to wanting.

"When I said get to know each other, I did not mean biblically," Fifi says loudly and with a cackle from the doorway.

We spring apart. Fifi cackles more.

"Danceball is only six weeks away. Is time to get serious."

We practice for two hours straight. By the end, X and I are both sweaty and exhausted.

"That was best practice yet. Chemistry is much better," she says with a wink. "But unfortunately, need more than chemistry to win."

She sets us a grueling practice schedule. Mondays are for bachata. Tuesdays are for salsa. Wednesdays for West Coast swing. Thursdays for the Hustle. Since Argentine tango is the hardest, she schedules three days of practice: Friday, Saturday and Sunday.

After we agree to the schedule, she claps her hands together. "Now is time to see what you two are really made of," she says.

CHAPTER 36

Salsa Tuesday

<Tuesday, 12:13 AM>

X: Fifi is not in her right mind

Me: More caliente! More caliente!

Me: I think caliente is the only Spanish word she knows

X: How many times do you think she said that?

Me: Fifty or sixty

X: Maybe more

X: So I'm reading that book you told me about

Me: Which one?

X: Cupcakes and kisses

X: I wasn't expecting it to be so DIRTY

Me: You're at the first bakery scene

X: Frosting belongs on cake

Me: So narrow-minded you are

X: What are gorgeous mounds of flesh?

X: I didn't learn about that in bio

Me: They only teach that stuff 2nd semester senior year

X: Ouch

Me: Sorry

X: For real tho, I don't think this thing with the frosting is sanitary

Me: Goodnight X

X: Never going into a bakery ever again

Me: I'm sleeping now

X: Who even knows where those cookies have been

X: Secret sauce my ass

X: You still there?

Me: Yes, sorry. I was dying of laughter

X: I like making you laugh

Me: You're pretty good at it

———————

CHAPTER 37

West Coast Swing Wednesday

I'M FAST ASLEEP and dreaming when my phone chirps at me.

X: You up?
Me: Yes
X: Can I call you?
Me: Yes

My phone rings right away. "Hi," I say, trying to sound like I wasn't just fast asleep and dreaming.

It doesn't work. "Oh man, I woke you up," he says.

"No, it's okay," I say, blinking into the dark. "How are you? How'd your show go?"

"Show was fine," he says. He doesn't say anything for a while. I hear the rustle of his sheets and I tug my blanket up under my arms and nestle down into my pillows and wait for him to go on.

"My pops called. We got into it again," he says.

"About what?"

"Same thing we always argue about. How I'm throwing my life away with the music nonsense."

"I'm sorry, X."

"Yeah," he says. We slip into silence. It feels like we're lying side by side in a small boat floating down a dark and quiet lake.

"Want to know a secret?" he asks. His voice is scratchy and soft.

"What?"

"Sometimes I wonder if he's right."

I'm too surprised to say anything right away. I would never guess X has doubts about music, not from the way he talks about it and not from the way he is onstage.

"You remember when we were playing pool and you said when you found out about your dad's affair, it was like he betrayed your idea of who he was?"

"Yeah."

"I think maybe that's how Pops feels about me. Before Clay died, the band was just a hobby. Pops and me always had an understanding—nothing too explicit—that I'd go to college and major in something practical. After Clay died, though, everything changed for me. I started trying to make sense of the world and my place in it."

His voice is so quiet now I have to press my phone closer to my ear to hear him. "In the end all I could come up with was how much I loved playing guitar and singing and being onstage. I figured out that being in the band meant more to me than I thought it did. And once you figure out what you love the most, you don't really have time for anything else. I couldn't get Pops to understand that, though. I get why he's mad at me. I changed the rules on him."

I turn onto my side. My blinds are slightly open, and

moonlight makes long rectangles on the floor. "I'm gonna say something and you don't have to say anything back, but you can't get mad at me either. I'm just gonna put it out there."

"Okay, what?" he asks.

"I think you should finish high school."

For a while he doesn't say anything, and I think our little metaphorical boat on the lake is about to capsize. But then he starts to laugh. "Woman, I pour my heart out to you and you tell me to finish high school."

"Your heart is great. It really is. And I promise you, you're not wrong about music. I've seen you onstage. You were made for it. But also, just finish high school. You have one semester to go. Your dad will be a lot less mad at you, I promise."

His laugh turns into a low chuckle. "All right, my turn to say something that you can't get mad at me for."

"Oh boy."

"Don't worry. It's not that bad."

"Oh boy," I say again.

"I think you should try to work things out with your dad. I think you should go to his wedding."

Now our boat does capsize. I sit all the way up. "After what he did? Why would you say that?"

"Right after Clay died, I used to see him everywhere, but it was weird. I didn't see all the things we used to do. I kept seeing all the things we were *supposed* to do." He clears his throat. "That make sense?"

"You were missing the future you were supposed to have."

"Yeah, like I was having memories of things that never got to happen."

I think about Dad and all the stuff we don't get to do with each other anymore. It's the big things like playing pool, and it's the silly, small things too. Like the way he used to kiss my forehead at the kitchen table every morning. Or the way he played Ella Fitzgerald or Nina Simone on Sunday mornings. The way he would leave the kitchen cabinets open and drive Mom up the wall.

You can miss the future with people who are still alive too.

"Okay," I say. "I'll think about it." I try to stifle a yawn, but it comes out anyway.

"I should let you go to bed," he says. "Sorry I woke you up."

"Don't be sorry. You can wake me up anytime," I say. "Good night, X."

"Good night, Evie," he says.

CHAPTER 38

Hustle Thursday

<Thursday, 8:55 PM>

Me: You were good with the hustle today

X: I like it

X: It's basically disco dancing but with a partner

Me: That's a good way to put it

X: I didn't come up with that

X: I read it online somewhere

X: Trying to impress you with my dazzling insight

X: Did it work?

Me: Only a little

X: Ha!

X: So I was thinking maybe your friends would want to come see a show on Saturday

Me: Do I get to come too?

X: Nah, just your friends

Me: Hehe

X: So that's a yes?

Me: I'll ask them but I'm sure they'll say yes

Me: They like you

X: I like them too

\<9:38 PM\>

Me: I thought about what you said last night about dad
and the wedding

X: Yeah?

Me: I haven't decided what to do yet

Me: But I'm thinking about it

X: That's good

X: I'm thinking about what you said about school too

Me: And?

X: Still thinking about it

Me: That's good

————

\<12:05 AM\>

X: Reading cupcakes and kisses again

Me: Can't get enough huh?

X: The girl just said her guy smells like cinnamon
chocolate buttercream

Me: Very specific

X: What do I smell like?

Me: You're odorless

X: Nah

X: I smell like rock and roll

X: And man sweat

X: And the blood of my vanquished enemies

X: You there?

Me: Laughing

X: Take your time

————

CHAPTER 39

Argentine Tango Friday

ON FRIDAY, FIFI is dressed in full Argentine tango splendor: short, cherry-red asymmetrical dress complete with fringe. The fringe is also asymmetrical. Her shoes are red, high and strappy.

X wolf-whistles at her when he walks in. "You're hot fire today," he says.

She strikes a dramatic pose with her right hip jutted out and her left leg extended. Her facial expression is somewhere between *I want to kiss you* and *I want to murder you*. She meets my eyes in the mirror. "You will wear very similar outfit for competition," she says.

I protest. "It's a little short, Fifi."

"You have legs for it." It's a compliment *and* an order.

Beside me, X just kind of laughs into his fist.

"Now," she says, clapping her hands together. "Argentine tango is my favorite dance in all the world. It is seductive. It is sorrowful. It is sensual." *Zeductive. Zorrowful. Zensual.*

X looks at me, laughter dancing in his eyes. I slap my hand over my mouth so I don't have a giggling fit.

"My first tango instructor say he would spend his last three minutes on earth dancing the tango. When you two feel like that, then you know you are ready."

"Damn, Fi, that's a lot of pressure," X says.

"That is tango," she says. She stomps her foot. "Now, we get started."

She positions us in the center of the studio a few feet away from the front mirror. "First thing to know is that hold is closed," she says, and adjusts our arms. Once she's satisfied with that, she circles and corrects us until our spines are straight but tilted slightly toward each other. "Now you put chests together."

My heart takes off at full speed. I'm not sure where it's going.

Next she moves us on to the tango walk, which is more a dramatic glide than a walk. In a normal walk, your heel touches first, then the middle, then your toes. In the tango walk, it's the opposite.

"Other thing to know is that tango is dance of improvisation. I will teach you steps and techniques, but you have to put them together when you dance. You have to feel."

She faces the mirror and begins swaying to a song in her head. "X, when you dance you must lead her into her passion. You must seduce her mind with your body so that she is yours for the taking. And Evie, you must give yourself to him—"

"That's totally sexist," I say.

She waves me off. "Yes, of course. That is tango," she says again.

We practice for two hours. Fifi alternates between praising my technical skills and lamenting my inability to "give in to passion of music."

"Tango is dance of desire. For the three minutes of tango, there is nothing else but him. While you are dancing, you belong to him."

"Once again, totally sexist," I say.

"To be desired is also powerful, no?" she says.

I don't know about that.

But the truth is, I understand what she's saying. I *am* holding myself back. I *am* afraid to give in completely to how I feel about X.

"Not to worry," she says to me as we're leaving. "Tango comes for everyone. You will learn to let go eventually."

CHAPTER 40

Declarations

"YOU GUYS WERE way better than I thought you'd be!" Cassidy shouts to X, Jamal and Kevin after their show.

X laughs. "I'll take that," he says, grabbing extra chairs for the table.

Kevin and Jamal give Cassidy a *who the hell are you, white girl?* look that she shrugs off.

"Don't listen to Cassidy," Sophie says. "You guys were great."

"This was my first rock and roll show," says Martin, sounding like someone's great-great-great-grandparent from another planet. "It was incredible."

X does the introductions and makes his way around the table to me. His eyes are doing that electric, glittering thing I noticed the first time I saw him play. He tugs me to my feet and then picks me up and twirls me around. I yelp and hold on tight while he laughs into my hair.

"We do okay?" he asks.

"Amazing," I say.

He smiles against my neck, and his dreads are softly scratchy against my cheek.

I press myself closer. There's a feeling inside me like a balloon that's one breath away from bursting. We've spent so much time together lately, just the two of us: dancing, texting, talking until way too late into the night. It feels good to be out with our friends, but it feels like a big step too. Like we're making a public declaration to his friends and mine.

I feel like I'm making a declaration to myself. Despite what the visions have taught me, I'm still doing this thing with X.

X sits down in my chair and I sit on his lap. He wraps his arms around my waist. Everyone's talking and laughing, but I'm barely listening. The club is even darker and smaller and smellier than I remember. I think maybe their cleaning products are actually made from stale beer and pee. The main act is getting set up onstage, and the club fills with even more people. X laughs at something, and I feel the rumble of it against my back. I love the way he laughs, free and open and with all of himself.

After a while Jamal and Kevin take off. They have dates with some "lovely concertgoers," as Jamal puts it. X fist-bumps them both goodbye. I watch the two of them disappear into the arms of a group of outrageously hip people.

None of us wants the night to end, so we end up back at Cassidy's house. As usual, her parents are away, on location for a movie shoot. She takes us out to their "outdoor entertaining area." It's more like a miniature country club than a backyard, and it's beautiful. My favorite part is the blue-green lazy river that bubbles and meanders up and through the sloping lawn. Café lights flicker overhead, strung between tall, wide palm trees. There's a full bar, couches, love seats and even a gas fireplace filled with bright-blue glass and lava rocks.

Cassidy turns on the fireplace and gets us all drinks from the bar. Something about a fire makes you want to stare into it. For a few minutes we sit there watching the flames while listening to the bubbling of the pool and the rush of the Santa Ana winds through the palm trees.

"My parents never, ever come out here," Cassidy confesses into our silence.

Sophie tips her head onto Cassidy's shoulder, and Cassidy takes a sip of whatever she's drinking.

"Thanks for inviting us," X says. "Hands down the nicest damn house party I've ever been to."

She laughs. "It is fabulous, right? I'm glad you guys came."

Martin's sitting in the single armchair across from me and X. He nudges me with his foot. "Did you really write that 'Black Box' song?" he asks.

Right before the band launched into it at the show earlier, X told the audience that I'd written the lyrics.

"That one was my favorite," Sophie says.

"I only helped a little," I say.

X shakes his head. "She means a lot."

Everyone's eyes are on us, and I'm more than a little self-conscious.

Cassidy gets a mischievous gleam in her eye that tells me she's going to embarrass me. "Aww, you guys are so cute," she teases.

"Aren't we, though?" X says back, refusing to be embarrassed.

Martin stands up suddenly. "I have a declaration to make." He clears his throat. "The next time Danica is single, I'm going to ask her out."

"Good for you, man," X says, clapping. "I hope she says yes."

I feel a pang of worry, but I force it aside. After all, here I am with X, risking an unknown future.

"I hope she says yes too," I say.

I've surprised Martin. "I thought you'd try to talk me out of it," he says.

"Evie's growing," Cassidy says, laughing and raising her glass into the air.

"Can I make a declaration too?" Sophie asks.

"Of course, babe! Declarations all around."

"I declare that one day I'll be on the International Space Station."

Then it's Cassidy's turn. "I declare . . . a thumb war," she says. We all laugh and try to get her to be serious and actually declare something, but she's not having it.

Now it's my turn. "Do I have to stand?"

Both Martin and X say yes at the same time.

"Fine," I say, getting up. "I declare that I'm going to my dad's wedding."

"No. Way," says Martin.

"Yes way," I say, nodding.

"That's too much growth," says Cassidy.

"I'm proud of you, Eves," Sophie says.

X just smiles at me. "Guess it's my turn," he says, standing up. "I declare that one day I'll be in the Rock and Roll Hall of Fame. I also declare that I'm going to finish high school. Someday soon. Ish."

We all laugh.

"Speaking of high school," Martin says, "I can't believe it's almost all over."

"Don't you dare get sentimental!" Cassidy yells. She's more than a little tipsy now. "Besides, we still have our summer road trip."

My vision of Sophie and Cassidy and their breakup and what it means for our road trip rises in my head, but I push it back down. Martin gives me a quick look to see how I'm doing. I flash him a smile that says I'm fine. I press my shoulder into X and remind myself that I'm living in the moment.

Cassidy pours herself another glass of wine. "You know what this party needs? Music," she says. She does something on her phone and suddenly music is coming out of speakers I can't see. She springs up. "Come on, show us some of that fancy ballroom dancing."

"Noooo, let's just sit here," I say. "Besides, we can't ballroom to this." I bury my face in X's shoulder.

But X isn't having it. He tells Cassidy what music to play and suddenly we're giving impromptu dance lessons. We start with bachata. Somewhat surprisingly, Sophie and Martin get infinity hips right away. Cassidy takes a longer time. We move on to salsa and then to the Hustle, trading partners so Martin doesn't feel like a fifth wheel.

We drink more and dance more and we're loud and tipsy

and silly and all so in love with each other it makes me want to laugh and cry at the same time.

Happiness is tricky. Sometimes you have to fight for it. Sometimes, though—the best times—it sneaks up behind you, wraps an arm around your waist and pulls you close.

CHAPTER 41

Joy Emoji

<Thursday, 9:47 AM>

Me: Hey Dad

Dad: Hi, honey. Is something wrong?

Me: Everything's fine

Me: I have something to say

Me: But I just want to say it over text

Me: If I talk I'll cry and I don't want to cry

Dad: Okay.

Me: I decided to come to your wedding

Dad: That's wonderful. You don't know how happy it makes me to hear that.

Me: Yeah ok

Dad: Are you sure I can't call you? Texting is a poor medium for conveying joy.

Me: God you're such a nerd dad professor

Me: Please don't call. I get how happy you are

Dad: Okay, sweetheart.

Dad: You know Shirley's shower is next Sunday. Would I be pushing it to ask you to go to that too?

Me: Yes that's definitely pushing it

Me: But I'll go

Dad: !!!!!!!!!!!!!!!!

Me: That's a lot of exclamation points dad

Dad: It really is such a poor medium for communication.

Me: You gotta get some emojis in there

Dad: Not in a million years.

Dad: I love you very much, Evie.

Me: ❤ ❤ ❤

———

❀

CHAPTER 42

Uncomfortable Silences

SHIRLEY'S WEDDING SHOWER is "themed," which is a fancy way of saying it's a costume party. We're supposed to dress like we're going to afternoon tea at Buckingham Palace.

For the occasion, Danica's wearing some sort of vintage, sleeveless, pink-and-white-flower-patterned silk dress. She's also wearing an elaborate hat sculpture. I see a hummingbird and hibiscus flowers nestled in her Afro. It sounds ridiculous but looks incredible. Choosing the perfect outfit for every occasion is her superpower.

My outfit is nothing special, just a beige skirt and a gauzy pale-yellow blouse. I (briefly, very briefly) considered wearing funeral black. I've talked myself out of going to this thing at least two times in the past week. Both times, X talked me back into it.

Mom's at the kitchen table, drinking tea and flipping through yet another recipe book when we get downstairs. She closes the book and presses one hand over her heart when she sees us. I'm not sure I understand the look she's giving us. There's pride there, and something else too.

"When did you girls get so big?"

"Big *and* beautiful," Danica says with a little curtsy.

"You were always beautiful," she says. "But I just don't know when you got so big." She sounds genuinely surprised—astonished, even—like we grew two feet overnight.

"You okay, Mom?" I ask.

"Yes, man. I'm fine," she says, waving me off. She walks over to Danica and adjusts the hibiscus on her hat. She dusts something I can't see off my shoulder.

"Time really flies, you know," she says. "And the older you get, the faster it flies."

I don't think the slight Jamaican accent I hear in her voice is my imagination. I scour her face for a sign that she's feeling less than fine, but I can't find one. But how can she be okay when she's sending us off to Dad's soon-to-be bride's wedding shower? How can she be so over it, when I'm not at all?

"You girls have a good time," she says, and sends us out the door.

————

The shower is forty-five minutes away at a hotel in Pasadena. When we get there, the other guests are easy to spot. Flower-patterned dresses and enormous hats abound. We get a few stares and even some double-takes from the staff and hotel guests. I suppose they don't see large groups of mostly Black women dressed for a garden party every day. That, or they're flabbergasted by our tremendous beauty.

The hostess leads us out to a courtyard patio, and it feels like we've stepped into a wild English garden. I see bougain-villea on trellises and climbing vines on the walls. Lavender, rosemary and jasmine bushes are everywhere. I see hibiscus, poppies and marigolds and other bright flowers I don't know the names of.

It's all very beautiful, like a fairy tale.

Shirley is the evil stepmother.

Obviously.

It's not hard to spot Shirley. She's the only one wearing a white veil instead of a hat. Danica makes a beeline for her. I watch them hug. Danica twirls to show off her outfit and Shir-ley claps her hands together, delighted. They look more like sisters than future stepmom and daughter. I try not to stare, but I can't help myself. The last (and only) time I saw her was when I caught her with Dad.

At least physically, she's nothing like Mom. Mom is tall and straight. Shirley is short and curvy. Mom has a short Afro. Shir-ley has a big wild one. I wonder if their personalities are differ-ent too. And if they are, then how did Dad manage to fall for both of them in one lifetime?

I force myself to stop staring and hurry to my table. If I can manage to avoid talking to Shirley for the entire shower, then today will have been a success.

As soon as I sit, my phone buzzes with a message from X. Just seeing his name on my screen makes me feel less panicky.

X: Doing ok? he asks.

I take a selfie holding one of the fancy teacups. I text it to him with the caption #teaforone.

He texts back immediately. *Want me to come join you?*

I'd love for him to be here. He'd make me laugh. He'd distract me from the sad, angry, panicked churning in my stomach.

Girls only, I text back.

Two minutes later, he sends me a picture of himself wearing a dress, heels and a lot of makeup.

I zoom in and decide he looks pretty great. I have many questions about the picture but not enough time to ask them.

Danica arrives at the table with Aunt Collette (Dad's older sister) and Cousin Denise (Collette's daughter). They live in San Francisco, so we don't see them a lot. Aunt Collette spends ten minutes telling me and Danica how she can't believe how grown-up we are. Danica and I smile at each other. First Mom and now Aunt Collette. Why are grown-ups constantly surprised that we kids grow up? I'm pretty sure that's what we're supposed to do.

After a few minutes, waiters descend to take our tea orders and the shower begins in earnest. The garden fills with the buzz of twenty-something women chatting and celebrating.

Shirley is at the next table over, sitting with five women. Again, I can't help watching her. A couple of the women look like her sisters, with the same wide eyes and high cheekbones. The older woman sitting right next to her must be her mom. She's what Shirley will look like in thirty years. Her mom leans over and whispers something into her ear that makes her throw her head back and laugh. Shirley's laugh is loud and strangely dolphin-esque. It's also completely contagious. I can't help smiling.

"There goes baby girl with that laugh," says a hooting older woman at another table. A few other people chuckle along.

I make myself stop gawking at her. Even her laugh is different from Mom's. Mom laughs like she doesn't want to disturb the air. Shirley laughs like a tornado. For the millionth time, I wonder if Dad fell out of love with Mom first or if he fell in love with Shirley first. If Shirley didn't exist, would our family still be together? Or would he just have fallen for someone else?

Fortunately, the waiters descend on us again, saving me from pondering questions with unknowable answers. This time, they're carrying tiered silver trays filled with tiny sandwiches and miniature desserts. I hear a lot of oohing and aahing. One woman says she hopes they're bringing more food.

Danica takes artful pictures of everything she eats and posts them. I take less artful pictures and text them to X.

I send him a photo of a tiny lemon custard pie complete with a gold leaf lying on top. He sends a single potato chip sitting in the center of one of Maggie's china plates.

I send him one of a triangular salmon sandwich topped with caviar. He sends me one of a dollop of jam surrounded by four bread crusts.

We go on like this and I laugh my way through the entire meal.

Forty-five minutes later, I've eaten as many cucumber sandwiches and scones with clotted cream as any person reasonably should. I tried not to like the food, but it was completely delicious.

Finally, it's time for the actual gift exchange part of the

event. Mentally, I prepare myself for boredom. And I'm not wrong. It *is* spectacularly boring. Mostly it consists of Shirley opening presents, cooing over the present and then tearfully thanking the giver of the present. Fifteen presents in, I want to stab myself. Twenty presents in, I do stab myself. I'm kidding.

After the last present is opened and ritually appreciated, Shirley's mom stands up and clinks her fork on her champagne glass.

Someone yells out, "Don't you make us cry now, Ms. Gene."

"Oh, you know she will," someone else shouts back.

Ms. Gene shushes them both. "You all just be quiet now." She turns to Shirley, takes her hand and kisses it before turning back to us.

"For those of you who know my Shirley, you know she's been through a lot." She stops talking and puts her fist over her heart. "Some of the things she's been through, no one should have to endure. I don't know why the Good Lord saw fit to put her through all that, but He works in mysterious ways."

Shirley bows her head slightly and her sisters cover her hands with theirs.

What has she been through? I wonder.

Her mom leans down to kiss her forehead. When she straightens back up, she's crying. "I promised myself I wasn't going to cry on this beautiful day, but . . . Anyway, today is not about old pain. Today is a celebration."

A chorus of *mm-hmm*s goes up around the room.

"When Shirley first told me she met a man . . . let's just say I was skeptical."

Another round of *mm-hmm*s and laughter.

I sit up straighter. It's weird hearing someone else talk about Dad like he belongs to them.

"But I said to Shirley that I would keep my mind open when I met him. And when I did meet him, I told him I was going to be hard to please." She smiles down at Shirley. "But, miracle of miracles, he pleased me. First of all, he's a good man. A family man. I'm so glad to have two new grandchildren to fuss over."

She smiles over at our table and raises her glass to Danica and me.

I raise my glass of sparkling cider, and Danica raises hers too.

It's only been a few minutes, but I can already tell that Shirley's mom is the kind of person who loves big. She's proud and fierce and sweet too. It's obvious how much she loves Shirley. It's obvious that she'll love me and Danica big too.

There's a part of me that would like to get to know her, that would like to feel the weight of that big love. But another part of me resents being claimed. My family was just the right size before. I already have two actual grandmothers. I don't need another one. I don't *want* another one. And I know what I'm feeling isn't exactly fair, but that doesn't make it any less true.

Shirley's mom keeps going: "And you should see the way he looks at my Shirley, like she put the sun and the moon and all the stars in the sky. It's almost embarrassing the way he loves her. But a love like that is what she deserves."

I want to protest. Dad loved Mom like that too, didn't he? Where did all his love for her go? Did it just disappear? Did he transfer it all to Shirley? Is that how love works?

"And you know my Shirley loves with her whole heart. She just dotes on him and his ten-dollar English-professor words. So now I want everybody to raise those glasses high. Yes, yes, get them up there." She looks down at Shirley. "Sweetheart, you are the love of my life. I'm so glad you found the love of yours."

Tears are streaming down Shirley's face, and she doesn't try to wipe them away. Her face is so full of love for Dad, it's almost hard to look at. I've thought a lot of awful things about her over the last year. I've called her a liar and a cheat. I blamed her for taking Dad away from us. And for making things awful between Mom and me and Danica and me. I've been angry. So angry.

But looking at her now, I see how much she loves Dad. Of all the things I expected to feel today, understanding for Shirley wasn't one of them. It's hard to completely hate someone who loves someone you love. She loves Dad. I can't deny that. Just like I can't deny that I still love him.

Danica's crying too. I don't know if she's feeling conflicted or overwhelmed like I am. I reach over and squeeze her hand. She squeezes back, and then it's all too much for me. Too many emotions swirling together inside me. Too many emotions that are half one thing and half another. Too much beauty and too much sadness.

I squeeze Danica's hand again but then let go of it and bolt from the table. By the time I get to the bathroom, I'm crying just as hard as Danica and Shirley were. I hide in one of the stalls and let my tears fall.

I don't know how much time goes by, but eventually I'm

not crying so much anymore. In the mirror I fix my tear stains and mascara smudges as best as I can. I text Danica to tell her I'm in the bathroom and that she should come get me when she's ready to go. I don't trust myself not to cry again in front of everyone.

Less than twenty seconds later, the door swings open. I turn around fast, hoping it's Danica and we can get out of here and go home.

But it's not Danica.

It's Shirley.

She takes a searching look around the room until she finds what she's looking for.

And what she's looking for is me.

"There you are," she says, sounding relieved. She walks over to where I am at the sink. I see the moment she realizes I've been crying. "I was hoping we could talk," she says, relief gone from her voice.

"I don't know if that's such a good idea."

She nods like she understands. "Don't worry. I'm not going to ask you to forgive me. I know that's too much to ask."

I relax a little, knowing that.

She takes a deep breath. "I want to thank you for deciding to come to the wedding."

I don't know what I was expecting, but it wasn't this. "I'm not doing it for you," I say.

"I know, but thank you anyway."

She closes her eyes for a quick second and takes another deep breath, gearing up for something.

I wrap my arms around myself. I'm not sure I'm emotionally ready for anything else today.

"There's another thing I want to say," she says. "I'm sorry for the way things happened between me and your dad. And I'm sorry that this is hurting you. I love your dad. I know you might never like me, but I already love you because you're a part of him."

I don't know what to say, so I don't say anything.

Her eyes roam across my face, looking for something. "You're so much like him," she says with a smile. "He's real good with uncomfortable silences too."

She turns around to face herself in the mirror. "I'm terrible at it. All I want to do is talk and talk and talk to make it better." She laughs and adjusts her veil. "I'm doing it right now, I guess."

"A little," I say with a small smile.

There's hope on her face when she turns to me again. But I drop my eyes from hers. I can't make any promises. I'm not ready for that, not yet.

"Thanks for coming today, Evie. It's really nice to see you," she says.

———

Danica's mostly quiet for the entire cab ride home. She doesn't even look at her phone.

I stare out the window and think about all the visions I've seen in the last few months. It occurs to me that an unhappy ending for one person can mean a happy beginning for another, the way Mom's unhappy ending with Dad led to Shirley's happy beginning with him. I think about the way we're all just starring in our own stories.

In her speech, Ms. Gene made it sound like Dad rescued Shirley somehow. In her version of things, Shirley's not the evil stepmother that I think she is, that I *thought* she was. She's the princess who finally found her prince.

"What did you think?" I ask Danica when we're almost home.

"I thought it was beautiful," she says.

"Me too," I say. And I mean it. It was beautiful. But it was sad too. Both things, and at the same time. I don't know why so much of life is like that.

CHAPTER 43

Entertain Us

LA DANCEBALL IS only four weeks away now, and Fifi steps up our practice schedule from rigorous to outlandish. Instead of two hours, our weekday sessions are now three. She takes us back to the promenade to see how well we can attract an audience and keep their attention. She makes us teach mini dance lessons to strangers, and then dance with the strangers. "Best way to learn is to teach," she says.

The extended practice sessions improve our salsa, bachata, Hustle and West Coast swing. But the Argentine tango is still a beast. Mostly it's my fault. At least, according to Fifi it's my fault. "You need to be more sensual and loose," she tells me. "Let yourself be swept away."

And I *am* trying. I have the steps down cold. X's lead is stronger now, and I'm better at following it. But I still can't manage to relax. For the tango, I'm supposed to give myself to X as if I can't help myself. But I'm afraid that if I pretend even for three minutes, I won't be able to stop. The truth is, I don't want to stop. And even though I'm seeing fewer visions these days because I know how to avoid them, I'm still afraid of what the future holds for us.

Now that I'm friends with my friends again, X slips into our little group as if he's always been a part of it. He goes with me to all our beach bonfires. He brings his guitar and we sing silly songs and play Tipsy Philosophicals. We go to his shows as a group. Cassidy drinks too much and blames it on the music. Groupies are supposed to party, she says. Martin nicknames us X Faction.

As spring gets hotter, we decide to spend Sunday mornings at Cassidy's house by the pool instead of at Surf City Waffle. The first time X takes his shirt off to get into the pool, I nearly die. I look so hard that I trip over my own feet and almost knock myself out on the lip of the pool. For the rest of the day I'm convinced I've stumbled into one of my romance novels. How else to explain how ridiculously hot his whole chest-abs-stomach combination is? X without a shirt is very nearly fatal.

At three weeks to go before the competition, Fifi changes our schedule again. We go from outlandish to fantastically, breathtakingly unreasonable. Four hours of practice a night instead of three. She cares not at all about my social calendar, homework or home life.

"Dance *is* life!" she says.

At two weeks to go, she begins videotaping every practice. She makes us watch our performances while she critiques them as if we're not in the room.

The last week before the competition, she adds full dress rehearsals to the four hours of practicing.

When I get to the studio on Monday for our first dress rehearsal, X isn't there, but Fifi, Archibald and Maggie are. The three of them have set up folding chairs in the back next to the windows.

Only after hugs and kisses does it occur to me why they're here. "Are you going to judge us?" I ask, horrified.

Fifi answers. "Not judge. We are audience. You will entertain us."

Somehow that answer is more horrifying.

"I'll go change," I say, and get the hell out of there.

Studio two doesn't have a class tonight, so I use it to change. I unwrap my costume from its garment bag and love it all over again. It's an emerald-green, sequined, spaghetti-strapped dancer's dream. In a previous life, this dress was a mermaid princess. I shimmy my way into it, very careful not to mess up my braids, which are held up by approximately seventy-seven bobby pins. I check to make sure my heel protectors are on before strapping on my sparkly gold shoes.

Once everything is on, I face the mirror to get the full effect.

The full effect is . . . not bad.

The dress is fitted close, but not too tight. Except for the spaghetti straps, my shoulders and arms are bare. It feels like I have an ocean of skin, all of it glowing brown from the Sunday mornings at Cassidy's pool. Hopefully the judges don't mind tan lines. I examine myself from all angles and decide I like the way my body looks, curvy and strong. I lean closer to the mirror. Dance competition makeup is supposed to be theatrical and unsubtle. I've done an okay job, but Danica would've done it better.

When I get back to the studio, X is still not there. Archibald and Maggie coo at me, telling me I look beautiful. I'm in the middle of executing a perfect spot turn when X finally does walk in.

It's a testament to Fifi's relentless training that I don't stumble, because X right now is my own personal earthquake. He belongs on the cover of a romance novel about bad-boy rockers with hearts of gold. He's wearing black suspenders with smoothly tailored black pants. It turns out I really like suspenders.

I drag my eyes up to his face and realize he's looking at me the way I'm looking at him.

"Jesus God, Evie, you look fucking—"

Maggie cuts him off before he can finish. "Xavier Darius Woods, watch your language," she scolds.

In her entire life, no one has ever dared to shush Maggie, but I almost do it. I look fucking *what?*!

X rubs the back of his neck. "Sorry, Grams," he says, but he doesn't take his eyes off me.

"You look nice too," I say.

Fifi claps. "Positions!"

X and I take our places, and Fifi hits play.

Five dances and twenty minutes later, we're done. Archibald and Maggie marvel at how much we've improved.

"Westside Dance won't know what hit them," Maggie chuckles.

In her mind, she's already making room for the Top Studio Amateur trophy.

Since she's "just audience member" today, Fifi will only

say she enjoyed our performance. She tells us to go home and get rest.

X is getting his guitar from the closet when I break down and ask him. "What word were you going to use before?"

He knows exactly what I'm talking about. He turns around, giving me his full attention. *"Astonishing,"* he says.

Then he puts the whole sentence together. "Jesus God, Evie, you look fucking astonishing."

It's because I'm thinking about looking "fucking astonishing" that I don't notice Archibald and Maggie are still in the studio. It's why I don't notice the way they're leaning into each other.

Why I don't notice they're about kiss until it's too late.

And I see.

CHAPTER 44

Archibald and Maggie

BRIGHT MIDDAY SUNSHINE on a studio lot. A line of dancers, all of them Black men and women, holding portfolios and waiting for something. They're dressed head to toe in fluorescent spandex, with neon sneakers.

One of the dancers is Maggie, but a much younger version of her. Her face is clear and open, no wrinkles along her forehead, no gray at her temples. Instead of dreadlocks, her hair is braided and laced through with silver threads.

"This is the third audition we've been at together," says a voice from somewhere behind her.

Maggie turns to the voice. "Is that so?" she says to the young man she finds smiling at her. She raises a cool eyebrow. "I don't remember you."

A young Archibald falters and looks down at his feet, unsure what to say next.

Some of the women surrounding Maggie snicker.

A man wearing neon-purple spandex says, "Brother man, you have to come better than that."

Archibald straightens, recovers himself. "Listen, I just don't want you to be the one that got away."

Maggie unarches her brow, considers him for a long moment. "Best not let me get away, then," she says as her name is called to audition.

Television-blue light splashed across a group of smiling brown faces crowded into a small living room. Maggie is sitting in Archibald's lap. His arms circle her waist. Her arms rest on top of his.

"There! There he is!" Maggie screams, pointing at the screen.

The friends lean in closer, picking out Archibald from the group of background dancers in the music video.

Archibald doesn't bother looking at the TV. Instead, he holds Maggie even tighter. "I love you," he says.

Maggie twists, throws her arms around his neck. "I love you too," she says, and they topple over backward onto the ground.

Nighttime in a silver-tinseled ballroom. Archibald and Maggie are dancing the Viennese waltz.

Archibald is wearing a tuxedo.

Maggie's wedding dress is chiffon and lace.

They spin again and again into each other's arms.

They are made of joy.

A pale-green hospital room in the not-quite morning. Archibald and Maggie are lying together on the bed.

Maggie is holding a small swaddled bundle in her arms. "Look what we made," she whispers to Archibald. "Look at this beautiful thing we made."

A small kitchen with fading yellow sunlight leaking in through the blinds. Archibald and Maggie are sitting at a table, a worry of bills between them.

"I'm going to take that substitute teaching job," Archibald says.

Maggie shakes her head. "I don't want you giving up your dreams."

Archibald pushes the bills to one side, clears a path for his hand to take hers. "I already have my dreams, Mags."

Almost midnight in another pale-green hospital room. Maggie is sitting upright in her bed. On her face is a mixture of exhaustion and elation.

Archibald is holding their toddler-daughter in his arms.

"Remember," Maggie says to the little girl. "Hearts grow bigger so you can love more."

The little girl nods, kid-solemn, and doesn't take her eyes off her baby brother.

Archibald steering Maggie down a long, dark hallway. She's blindfolded and taking small, careful steps. Archibald guides her into a dance studio. The floors need finishing, and there's a panel missing from the back wall of mirrors.

"Just what are you up to, Archibald Johnson?"

"You ready to find out?" Archibald asks as he undoes her blindfold.

Maggie gasps and presses her fingertips over her heart. She spins in place. "Oh, Archibald," she says. "What did you do?"

"Time to start up those dreams again," he says.

This moment right now, the two of them sharing a small kiss in their studio.

A wide-open field and a coffin being lowered into the ground. It's snowing so lightly the flakes dissolve before they touch the ground. Maggie and Archibald lean into each other. "This isn't right," Archibald says to Maggie. "We're not supposed to be here."

Nighttime in an old-fashioned bedroom.

Older versions of Archibald and Maggie are lying on their bed. Archibald is on his back, his right arm wrapped around Maggie.

Maggie is lying on her left side. Her head is tucked into the crook of Archibald's neck. Her right cradles his chest.

The room is dim with amber light. The source of light is not obvious.

The air surrounding them is undisturbed by breath.

CHAPTER 45

The Invention of Language

DAD USED TO say that there was a word for every emotion, but I don't think he's right about that. I don't have a single word for the way Archibald and Maggie's vision makes me feel. Wonder and fright and astonishment and joy and terrible strange sadness and blossoming hope.

Love is too small, too singular a word for the feeling it's trying to hold. Just one word isn't enough, so I want to use them all. Sometimes I think love is the reason language was invented.

When Archibald and Maggie met in that audition line, they had no idea what they were at the beginning of. They didn't know that their love of dancing would make a place for others to love it too. Or that their love would branch out into the world and make children and then grandchildren. Or that their love would lead to mine.

Maybe the whole point of love is to make more of itself.

I try to fall asleep so I'll be ready for Danceball tomorrow, but the vision won't leave me. It plays in my head all night. I watch as Maggie and Archibald begin their lives together in the audition line a thousand times. I watch as they die together in bed a thousand more. I laugh through the happy parts of their lives and cry through the sad ones. Sometimes I do the opposite.

Martin said I was supposed to learn a lesson from my super-power. Is the Archibald-and-Maggie vision the lesson? Maybe what I'm supposed to learn is how big and strong love can be, and how long it can last. Their vision is the only one I've ever seen that doesn't end in heartbreak. Not every couple is Mom and Dad.

I fall asleep thinking about the fact that even though I've been trying to deny it, I'm in love with Xavier Darius Woods, and I have been for a while now.

CHAPTER 46

Danceball

DANCEBALL SATURDAY FINALLY arrives. X and I were up talking on the phone, so I only get two hours of sleep before my alarm wakes me up at six-thirty. If Fifi figures out I haven't gotten a full night's rest, she'll kill me with her stilettos.

By the time I'm showered and dressed, I feel more awake. Unfortunately, I don't *look* as awake as I feel. I poke at the dark circles under my eyes for a few seconds before deciding I need professional help.

I knock on Danica's door three times, but she's either still asleep or ignoring me.

I ease open her door. "Dani," I whisper-shout.

She groans and buries her head under her pillow. "Go away."

"I'm sorry. I need makeup help."

She unburies herself and squints over at me. Her face is puffy and she's wearing her silk sleep cap, but somehow she still looks great. "I was having a really good dream," she says.

"Danceball is today and I didn't get any sleep and I look terrible."

She sits halfway up and plucks her phone from her nightstand. "It's seven twenty-three a.m., Evie. On a Saturday."

"I need you, Doctor Dani," I say.

She sits all the way up now. "Wow," she says, "you haven't called me that in forever."

It's true. It's been so long I can't actually remember the last time.

When Danica first discovered the wondrous world of makeup, I was the one she did all her experimenting on. I'd pretend to be a patient whose face needed (cosmetic) saving and she'd be the genius young surgeon, the only one with enough guts and talent to help me. She's made me into a '60s hippie love child, a '70s disco diva, an '80s bubblegum-pop star. I've been glam, metal, hip-hop, punk rock, goth and more.

I don't remember when we stopped playing or why.

"Can you save me, Doc?" I make my voice low and gravelly and clutch at my face, pretending to be sick.

She laughs and bounces out of bed to inspect my face. "It'll be close," she says, touching the dark circles under my eyes. "You're pretty far gone."

"Hey, it's not that bad," I protest.

"I'm sorry, but are you the doctor?"

"No," I grumble.

"All right, I think I can save you," she says.

She leads me to her vanity and goes to work on me.

Forty-five minutes later, she spins me around to face the mirror. "What do you think?" She dabs at my cheek with one of her sponges.

I lean close to the mirror and gawk at myself. "Dani, it's incredible."

Her eyes fly to mine, and I can see she's relieved that I like it.

I lean closer. Somehow Dani made me look bold but not garish. Also, I look like I've slept for as long as Sleeping Beauty.

When and why did I stop thinking it was cool that she's good at this? I stand up and throw my arms around her, glad my lack of sleep forced me to ask her for help.

"Oh my God, don't mess up your face," she squeals, surprised by my attack. She hesitates for a few seconds, but then she hugs me back.

"Thanks, Doc," I say. "You're the best."

"I know," she says.

———

Danceball is in the grand ballroom of the Seasons hotel. The theme is "Hollywood Glamour," which apparently means gold. Because there is gold everywhere. Gold streamers, towers of gold balloons, gold confetti on the ground. All the signage is written in gold cursive, including a huge banner that reads *Welcome to the 17th Annual Los Angeles Danceball Championships.*

My stomach does a nervous two-step and I squeeze Mom's hand. We make our way to the registration desk.

"A lot of you amateurs dancing today," says the lady checking me in.

"How many?"

"Twenty-three." She hands me my envelope and wishes me luck.

Twenty-three couples means there'll be two quarterfinal heats to determine who gets into the semis. I open my packet and check to make sure all our details are right. Age group: *Under 21*. Partnership Type: *Am-Am*. Category: *Bronze Newcomer*. Style: *Nightclub*.

As (bad) luck would have it, our couple number is also twenty-three. Since we have the highest number, X and I will be always the last ones called when the judges announce which dancers are moving on. *If* we get called.

X and I agreed to meet downstairs at the designated practice floor.

I spot him right away, leaning against the wall next to the practice room. He looks the opposite of how I feel. Relaxed. Confident.

I wave at him. He pushes off the wall and walks over to us.

"Nice to see you again, Ms. Thomas," he says to Mom.

"Well, don't you look wonderful," she says. "You boys should have to wear this sort of thing all the time."

He hooks his thumbs into his suspenders. "Not sure these are the next big thing for eighteen-year-olds, Ms. T," he says, grinning.

While they chitchat, I let my eyes travel all over him. He looks the same as he did in rehearsal yesterday, but somehow better. His black patent-leather shoes are shined to glistening. His shirt is perfectly pressed. But it's the top two buttons that snag my attention. They're unbuttoned, and for a second I see my fingers unbuttoning a third and a fourth, until—

"Evie, you ready for this?" he asks just as I'm getting to the fifth button.

Yes.

So, so ready.

"Yes," I say at a completely unnecessary volume.

Mom rubs my shoulder and leans in close. "I don't remember him being this cute," she whispers.

I shush her and sneak a glance at X's face, hoping he didn't hear her.

Mom gives me a hug and a kiss and wishes us luck before taking off to meet Archibald and Maggie and Fifi upstairs.

"Let's scope out the competition," I say.

Since the pros don't compete until nighttime, the practice room is packed with mostly young amateurs. Per capita, the only other place you can find more sequins or bow ties on teenagers is prom. X and I shuffle along the perimeter until we find a free spot.

"This is wild," X says as we watch our competition. I look for the couple from Westside Dance that Maggie said would be our main adversary. They're about our age and very, very obviously in love, given the way they can't keep their hands off each other. They'll have no trouble with the "give yourself to each other" part of the Argentine tango.

Finally, one of the organizers gives us the five-minute warning. Dancers for the first heat start heading out.

"We should go up to on-deck," I tell X, even though we're in the second of the two heats.

He nods but then doesn't move. Instead, he cups the back of his head with both hands.

"You're nervous," I tease.

"I'm not," he says.

I reach up and touch his elbow and gently tug his arm back down.

He captures my hand in his and threads his fingers through mine.

By the time we get upstairs, the heat one dancers are already competing in the main ballroom. Bachata music filters out through the closed doors. A few of the other heat two couples dance along with the music.

Thirty minutes later, the heat one dancers file out. They're sweaty and breathing hard but happy and relieved too. They wish us luck.

And then it's our turn.

As it turns out, ballroom competitions are not stately affairs. The fans are boisterous and partisan. As soon as we walk into the main ballroom, they start whistling and screaming out the numbers of their favorite dancers.

I hear a few loud calls for twenty-three. X and I scan the audience until we find our little cheering section in the second row on the right. They're all waving wildly. Except for Fifi. Fifi just gives us a small nod.

"Well, she's consistent," X says, laughing.

Up at the mic, the lead judge welcomes us and goes over the rules and the order of dance. Bachata followed by salsa, West Coast swing, Hustle and, finally, Argentine tango. "Have fun, and dance your hearts out," she tells us.

X and I start off nervous, but by the time we get to West Coast swing, we've settled down. As usual, the Argentine tango is our weakest dance.

The song ends. We take our bows and exit the floor.

"You think we did it?" X asks when we're back downstairs in the practice room.

"I don't know," I tell him honestly.

He rubs his chest and pretends to be wounded. "Ouch, my heart," he says.

Impulsively I press my hand over his heart, feeling the beat under my palm. "Not a thing wrong with your heart," I say, looking up at him.

It's not long before an announcement comes over the loud-speaker. "Dancers, please make your way back to the ballroom for results."

The audience hushes quiet as soon as the lead judge takes the mic. She thanks everyone and says that she wishes we could all move on to the next round. It takes her forever to read the numbers, but finally she gets to ours. We made it to the semi-finals.

X lets out a whoop and our little cheering section goes wild. "Yeah, twenty-three!" Archibald yells.

We only get a short time to celebrate, though. One hour later, we're all back in the main ballroom and in position, ready to dance for a spot in the finals.

X smiles down at me, definitely more relaxed than before.

"Don't get cocky yet," I tell him.

"I'll wait until we win," he says with a wink.

He's not the only one feeling more relaxed. The energy of the whole floor is different from before. The smiles are bigger, the atmosphere looser. The audience feels it too. They're even louder, screaming the numbers of their favorites.

The music starts, and we're off. I lose myself in the music for the first four dances. I hope the feeling will last until the Argentine tango, but it doesn't. My muscles tense as soon as the music starts. I concentrate too hard on X's lead. Instead of dancing the music, I'm dancing the steps again.

Still, it's not like we're bad. We make it through the rest of the dance without any technical errors. But I know if we don't make it to the finals, it'll be my fault.

The wait for results is longer this time. The judges need to score each couple for each dance. Only six couples will make it to tomorrow's finals.

We wait for an hour. There's a lot of pacing and back-of-the-head rubbing. I do the pacing. X does the back-of-the-head rubbing.

Finally, it's time for us to go back into the ballroom. I try to read our fate on the judges' faces, but nothing doing. I try to read our fate on Fifi's face, but nothing doing there either.

The lead judge gets on the mic. "Thank you, competitors. You were all wonderful. The judges would like to see the following dancers . . ."

The fourth number she calls is eleven. It's the happily in-love couple from Westside Dance, the ones who are so good at Argentine tango.

The fifth couple she calls is number eighteen.

Once the applause dies down, the judge gets back on the mic. She smiles an *I know something you don't know* smile.

I kind of want to dance on her grave.

"I bet you guys are just dying to find out who has the final spot," she says, teasing us all.

I *am* going to dance on her grave.

The audience hoots in agony.

X squeezes my fingers and smiles into my eyes.

I smile back into his and I don't look away, not even when the judge makes her announcement. "Congratulations to couple number twenty-three. You have a spot in the finals."

X pulls me into a hug.

"I told you," he whispers into my ear.

All around us, everyone cheers.

CHAPTER 47

Becomes a Sea

AFTER WE MADE it to the finals yesterday, Fifi took us back to the studio for one last practice.

"Technically they're not as good as you, but their tango is like sex," she said as soon as we got there.

She was talking about the Westside Dance couple.

"Like good sex," she clarified.

X looked at me. "Did you think she meant bad sex?" he asked, deadpan.

"You know," I said, also deadpan, "I wasn't sure."

She ignored us both and then made us dance for an hour, saying the competition was ours to lose.

———

X is already holding up the wall outside the practice room when I get there.

"What's with you getting to places on time these days?" I ask.

"Maybe you're a good influence on me," he says. He pushes off the wall but doesn't give me his usual smile.

"What's the matter?" I ask. "Nerves again?"

He shrugs. "It's nothing."

But I can see it's not nothing, so I say so.

"Just thinking about the future."

"The one ten minutes from now, or the future-future?" I ask.

"Future-future."

I start to tease him about living in the moment, when it occurs to me he might be talking about something more concrete.

"What's wrong?"

"Talked to my dad last night."

"Did you fight again?"

"No, wasn't like that. I told him I was thinking about finishing up school and he was really happy about it. He said he'd set it up so I could come home for the summer and get it done. Get my degree."

"*This* summer?"

He leans back against the wall and looks down at his feet. "Yeah."

And I know I told him he should get his degree, and he really should. But summer seems so close now.

I feel sick. The part of me that's been avoiding kiss visions pipes up. All relationships end.

Is this what happens to us? He goes home for the summer? Then, in the fall, I go to NYU and he picks up his life in LA, and we just fade away?

"Are you going to go?" I ask.

"I don't know," he says. "What do you think I should do?"

I know he's not asking me for advice.

"We could make it work," I whisper.

He lifts his head. "How?"

"I hear New York City has a pretty good music scene," I say.

He moves closer to me, but not close enough. "I've heard that too," he says.

"Think the guys will mind moving the band there?"

"Nah. They won't mind at all." He ducks his head so we're face to face. So there's no mistaking what we're saying to each other. We're promising each other a future.

"Am I moving too fast for you?" I ask, remembering how I said I wanted to take it slow two months ago.

He laughs. "No, you're going at a good speed now. I've been waiting for you to catch up to me." He holds out his hand for me to take. "Let's go win this thing," he says.

We follow the other dancers upstairs to the on-deck area. We can't stop smiling at each other. His smile makes me smile makes him smile makes me smile some more. A smile cascade. Smiles like falling dominoes.

The ballroom looks the same as yesterday, except our cheering section has gotten bigger. I see Mom and Martin and Sophie and Cassidy. And Dad—in my excitement yesterday, I invited him to come. They scream like banshees when they see us.

The lead judge begins her welcome announcement, but to be honest, I don't really hear what she's saying. X's eyes roam over my forehead and across my cheeks, settle on my lips and repeat the circuit. Forehead, cheeks, lips. He lingers on the lips. I can't help but lick them. He makes a sound I want to hear him make again.

The judge finishes her announcement.

The lights dim.

And finally, it's time.

We're just as good as we were yesterday. Maybe even a little better, now that we have more room on the floor to dance, and two other dances under our belts. We're breathing hard by the time we finish the Hustle. I know what's next, but fortunately there's not enough time for panic.

The judge makes the announcement. "And now, couples, for your final dance, Argentine tango."

Fifi says Argentine tango is a dance of passion and release. I know exactly what she means.

The music begins.

We start to dance. Except it doesn't feel like we're dancing. It feels like we're flying across the floor.

We do ochos and reverse ochos. Barrida. Media luna.

His fingers spread across my back between my shoulder blades. I dip down, then arch back up into him. I don't have to think about what steps come next.

We've been dancing this dance for a while now.

We're moving fast, and all I can think is *don't let me go, don't let me go, don't let me go.*

Finally, the song winds down. We stay with it, giving ourselves to each other, until the music ends.

For a second, there's no sound. Our eyes meet and a kind of certainty settles inside me. This thing between us could *last*.

The way I feel about him—the way I think he feels about me—has only gotten bigger and wider and deeper every day, the way a stream becomes a river becomes a sea.

"I love you," I say.

He smiles, and I've never seen a smile this enormous on anyone for any reason.

"I love you too," he says.

We lean into each other and kiss. I don't hold anything back.

And I see.

CHAPTER 48

X and Me

OVERHEAD LIGHTS FLICKER on, lighting up a mirrored room. In the room's center, there's a boy. He's frowning and riding slow circles on a bike much too small for him. His frown vanishes when he notices the girl in the doorway staring at him.

The girl at the doorway has a wide-open face she often wishes weren't quite so wide-open. It never hides much of what she's feeling: confusion, then curiosity, then interest, then an attempt to hide her interest.

"Umm," says the girl. She says it to disguise the sudden speed of her surprised heart.

"I'm guessing this is yours," says the boy, startled by the way it feels like he knew her once and now will again.

X and me on a double-decker bus touring the city.

When he looks out, he sees his future dancing out just before him, almost close enough to touch.

When she looks out, she sees the city she already knows, and the places she's already been and everything she's already lost.

* * *

X and me at Surf City Waffle, unexpected candlelight flickering all around us. We're trading a pen back and forth, writing and re-writing words to his song. It feels like learning to dance, the way we stop and start again until the words match the feeling we're trying to capture. It feels like discovery, the way I'm learning not just about him, but about myself too.

X and me kissing for the first time on the beach with the ocean so loud and all around us, it feels like it's inside us too.

X and me right now, so in love and kissing in a brightly tinseled ballroom.

X and me in a car driving east down a long empty highway lit only by our headlights and the moon. Tomorrow we'll be in Bryce Canyon, but for now we're just on our way. The radio is on and the windows are open and the night air is warm and close. Some-times the world is full of such abounding joy, it's hard to know what to do with it all.

X and me in a mostly dark hotel room. Moonlight sneaks in through the curtains that don't quite close.

There's only one bed. He kisses me and my hand slips under his shirt. His lips are on my neck.

"Are you sure?" he asks me before we go on.

"Yes, I'm sure," I say. "Yes."

Then we are nothing but hands and lips and wanting and having.

The world changes after that, the way colors surprise you after a rain.

Has the grass ever before been this green? Or that tree branch so black?

X and me in my small, dim dorm room. I'm holding my own guitar—the one he bought for me—in my hands.

"Show me what you've been practicing," he says.

I play the song I've been working on, "Miss the Future."

He kisses me after I'm done. "That was beautiful, and I'm not just saying that because I'm in love with you."

"I dunno," I say. "You do love me an awful lot."

"Come sing it onstage at our next show," he says.

At first I hesitate, but then I say yes. I wonder if being with him will always feel like discovery.

Me, alone, in a bedroom. It's nighttime and the lights are off.

My face and my chest and my ribs hurt. They hurt the way muscles do when you use them far too much for far too long.

I've been crying. I'm crying still.

I try to take a deep breath to calm myself, but it's painful. I try for a shallow one, but any amount of air is too much. A small breeze sighs across my face. I turn my head toward it. Streetlight through the open window paints a shadow on the floor. The edges are clear and they are sharp.

I look down at my hands and the thing I'm clutching between them.

It's a funeral program. There's a photograph of X's face. The caption reads *In loving memory: Xavier Darius Woods.*

The date on it is ten months from now.

CHAPTER 49

Gone, Part 1

APPLAUSE ROARS AROUND us. Because of our kiss, there are hoots and hollers too.

I rip myself away from X.

He reaches for me. "Evie, what's wrong?"

I back away and close my eyes against the confused hurt on his face when he realizes I'm running away from him.

Everything hurts. The air around me hurts.

I run and run until I'm gone from here. I run until I'm gone.

CHAPTER 50

Love and Its Opposite

I DON'T FEEL the wind through the open window of the cab. Or the soreness of my feet from my heels as I climb the stairs to my room. Or the throbbing of my scalp where my hair is pinned too tight. Or the scalding of the too-hot water against my skin. Or the slippery coolness of my sheets as I slide into bed. Or the warm tears on my face as I cry myself to sleep.

I don't feel anything at all.

The opposite of love isn't hate. It's death.

CHAPTER 51

Gone, Part 2

<Sunday, 3:31 PM>

X: Hey, where are you?

X: They're about to announce the winner

X: Where are you?

X: Holy shit we won

———————

< 4:05 PM>

X: Hey, been calling and calling

X: Why'd you take off like that?

X: You ok?

———————

< 6:08 PM>

X: Give me a call

X: Please

X: Let me know you're ok

Me: I'm here

Me: I'm fine

X: Just tried calling you

Me: I know

Me: I'm sorry. I can't explain

X: What's going on? Did I do something? Going too fast again?

X: I can slow down

Me: It's not that

Me: I just don't think this is going to work out

X: What's not going to work out?

Me: Us

X: I don't understand

X: You changed your mind about being together? About NY?

Me: Don't change your life for me

X: I want to change my life for you

X: I know the thing with your parents messed up how you feel about love

X: But what we have between us is going to work out

Me: No it won't

Me: I'm sorry

X: I don't understand. Are we breaking up right now?

Me: I'm sorry

———————

CHAPTER 52

Forgiveness

THE NEXT MORNING, Mom comes to my room and asks me for twenty minutes straight if I'm okay. She doesn't believe me when I tell her that I am.

Of course, she's right not to believe me. But I have no truth to tell her.

She says she tried to talk to me last night, but I was already asleep. She has a lot of questions: Why did I run away from the dance floor after X and I kissed? Did X hurt me?

I tell her he hasn't hurt me.

I tell her it was a goodbye kiss, but she says it didn't look like that to her. She says that to her, that kiss looked like hello.

I roll away from her and face the wall, wishing I were a stranger to her, to everyone. Right now, I don't want to be known. I don't want anyone to know anything about me at all.

I ask her to leave. Not in a mean way. But in a way that lets her know I need to be alone. She says okay, but not before making sure I know that she loves me.

Sometime later—maybe an hour, or maybe two, or maybe ten—I check my phone. Everyone has texted. Everyone has called.

Except X. Not that I expect him to. Not after I ran away from him. Not after I broke up with him over text. He doesn't call, and I don't want him to. It's better for both of us this way.

Over our group chat I tell Martin, Sophie and Cassidy that I'm fine and I'll see them at school.

When Martin texts separately, I tell him about my vision. I tell him X will die in ten months. I tell him I'm not ready to talk about it and I never will be.

I thank Maggie for her congratulations. I tell Dad I'm fine, totally fine.

Of all the texts, Fifi's is the one that almost gets me to feel something: *today I'm so proud of you. finally you dance with your heart.*

——

Mom lets me stay home from school for two days. By Tuesday night, she tells me I need to go back and face whatever it is I'm avoiding. She promises me it'll be better than staying home.

She turns out to be right. Going back to school keeps me busy. I tell Sophie and Cassidy that X and I had a fight and that we aren't together anymore. They want to know the details, but they understand that I'm not ready to talk about it yet.

Martin lets me call him and cry whenever I need to.

The rest of the week passes. The hardest time is just before I fall asleep, when the vision tries to slither its way into me. It tries, but I slam my mind shut. It's easier than I expected. According to Mom, the human body can do all sorts of amazing things, including pass out, to protect itself from pain.

The first Saturday after the competition, Mom comes to see me in my room before leaving for another date with Dr. Bob.

"Your father is on his way," she says.

I groan. "Why's he coming over here?"

She frowns and sits down on my bed. "I thought things were getting better between you two," she says.

I don't say anything. Things were getting better, but that was *before*. That was when I was starting to trust the world again. When I *wanted* to trust the world again.

"Besides," she says. "He's worried about you. We all are."

"I'm fine," I tell her.

She narrows her eyes at me and set her arms akimbo. "Have you showered today?"

I shake my head.

"Eaten?"

Another shake.

"Left the house?"

Her point is made.

She sighs. "I asked him to come over. He was always better at cheering you up when you were little."

It's true. Mom was always good for hugs and kisses after I hurt myself. But Dad was the one who made me laugh. And if I was laughing, then I wasn't thinking about the pain.

"I don't want to see him," I say.

"Too bad. He'll be here any minute now."

After she leaves, I go out to the patio. The sun has already set, and the air is slipping from warm to cool.

I don't want to remember X and me dancing to Indian music in this very spot, but that's not how memory works. Was that laughing, dancing girl really me? I don't recognize her. Just like I don't recognize the girl who used to read all the romance books and knew all the subgenres and believed in all the acronyms: One True Pairing (OTP) and HEA (Happily Ever After) and HFN (Happy for Now). Just like I don't recognize the girl who thought her dad could do no wrong. How many versions of me will there be in this one lifetime?

Dad rings the bell ten minutes later.

"I'm fine," I say to him, instead of hello.

He's wearing another pair of glasses I don't recognize. His goatee is now a full beard.

"I don't doubt you're fine," he says. "But let me check on you anyway." He shakes a take-out bag of Mariscos Chente at me.

"Thanks," I say, and lead him back out to the patio.

"This is nice," he says, taking a few steps out into the courtyard.

It takes me a moment to realize that he's never been out here before. He's never seen so much of this place where I live. How can our lives be so separate now?

I sit down in the armchair, tilt my head back and close my eyes. I can feel him studying me, deciding where to begin.

"Mom thought you could use some guffaw therapy," he says.

"I'm fine," I say without opening my eyes.

The chair across from me scrapes against the concrete as he sits down. "Sweet pea, you know you can tell me anything."

I open my eyes. "Why do you still call me sweet pea? You know I don't like it." I'm not angry. I'm just tired.

He rests his elbows on his knees and looks down at the ground. "You used to love it when you were little. There was a drawing you made of a pea that fell into a bowl of sugar." He shakes his head, but I think he's shaking it at himself. "I'm sorry. I'll remember not to call you that anymore."

He hands me a burrito. I'm not hungry, but I still eat half of it.

When he's done with his food, he leans back and wipes his hands. "So—" he begins.

But I stop him and ask the thing I've wanted to ask him for a year. "Why did you cheat on Mom?" I ask it so quietly I almost don't hear myself.

Watching his face is like watching clouds race across the sky. Guilt chasing sadness chasing shame.

For a long time he doesn't say anything, but then he does. "Your mother was the first woman I ever loved. We had you girls and we were happy for a long time." He covers his eyes with his hands. "But the last few years, things changed."

I almost wish I'd seen their vision. I'd love to know what they were like in the beginning. It'd be nice to have those memories.

He goes on. "Your mom and I weren't happy anymore."

"No," I say, "Mom was happy."

He closes his eyes but doesn't tell me I'm wrong. "Yes, your mother was happy. But I wasn't."

"But then why didn't you just tell her?" I ask, frustrated. "You could've gone to counseling or on more dates or something. Danica and I could've helped you."

"I made a lot of mistakes, Evie. You're right. I should've told her. I should've tried harder." He looks up at me for this next part. "And when Shirley came into my life, I should've walked away. But I didn't. And then it was too late. I couldn't come back from what I was feeling."

I've imagined having this conversation with him so many times, but I never expected him to admit that he made a mistake.

I'm more angry than frustrated now. He's my dad. He's not supposed to make these kinds of mistakes. "But you made vows to Mom. You promised her you'd love her forever."

"Evie, sweetheart, sometimes things change."

I'm so angry now, I'm incandescent with it.

"You promised her forever. You promised us, but you chose Shirley instead. You love her more." I know I'm not being fair and that I'm not making sense. All I want to do is smash things. I want to make it so no one and nothing can hurt me ever again. I want to get rid of every nice, kind, sweet, soft feeling inside myself until there's nothing at all. No joy, but no pain either.

"No, you're not allowed to think that. I love you and Danica more than I love anything else in the world," he says. "I'm sorry for what I did, but the thing I'm most sorry about is losing you."

Tears slip from my eyes. I don't try to wipe them away. There's so much more to come.

He pulls me into his arms and hushes me, the way he used to when I was small.

"Don't hush me," I say, jerking away from him. "What I want is for you to explain to me why people make promises to each other. Why bother to love people if they're just going to die and leave you all alone? You believe in God. Tell me why He would make the world like this. Tell me why He's so cruel."

I look at him and wait for him to give me some kind of answer because he's my dad and he's supposed to have the answers. He always used to.

He looks out into the blue-dark night, and it's a long time before he says anything.

Finally, his eyes travel over my face. "You're getting so big. I couldn't have imagined you would get this big." He looks out over the courtyard. "Here's what I think. If you get very, very lucky in this life, then you get to love another person so hard and so completely that when you lose them, it rips you apart. I think the pain is the proof of a life well lived *and* loved."

"That's a shitty answer," I tell him.

"Yes," he says. "It is."

I'm crying hard now, inconsolable. All I see is X's face on the funeral program.

In loving memory: Xavier Darius Woods.

In loving memory.

In memory.

"It's not worth it," I say.

Why do I have to love *him*? How am I supposed to live without him?

"I can't answer your questions, Evie. I don't know why we lose the people we love and how we're expected to go on after we lose them. But I know that to love is human. We can't help ourselves. The philosopher-poets say love is the answer, but it's more than that. Love is the question and the answer and the reason to ask in the first place. It's everything. All of it."

For a long moment, I watch the lights across the courtyard turn on and off and then on again. I wonder what's happening in each of the apartments. Who have they lost? Who are they about to lose? What have they survived?

Someone laughs high and loud. It sounds like something breaking. A small wind blows, and there's no warmth left in the air now. My tears dry on my face.

"Dad, I don't think I can go to your wedding after all."

I feel how much I've hurt him, and then I feel his struggle to accept what I've said.

"All right," he says.

"I don't know if I'm ever going to forgive you."

He drops his head into his hand. "It's all right, my sweetheart," he says.

Somehow the way he says it makes me feel like maybe I'm the one who needs forgiveness.

"It's all right," he says again.

And it's not all right, not really. But it's nice of him to say so.

CHAPTER 53

The Light and the Dark

WHEN I IMAGINE X dead, I don't see darkness. In darkness there's still hope. Some hidden thing in the places you can't see. Grief to me feels like an endless landscape of white light. No secrets. And no surprises either.

You can see clearly all you have lost.

Everything that's no longer there.

CHAPTER 54

One Million, Eight Hundred and Fourteen Thousand and Four Hundred Seconds

SOMETIMES THE ONLY thing to say about a period of time is that it's passing and that you're surviving it.

Graduation festivities kick into high gear. The yearbook comes out, and everyone, even the most jaded and cynical kids, turns nostalgic and earnest. We reminisce, sign each other's books and make promises we really want to keep.

Cassidy's parents go away to Europe, so she throws some kind of party almost every night. I go to all of them.

At my request, we start going back to Surf City Waffle. I have too many memories of X by the pool at Cassidy's house to want to go there anymore.

Every Sunday, I wonder if this is the Sunday when Sophie and Cassidy will break up. Things between them have been getting slowly worse. They smile less and touch less and bicker more.

Martin notices, but we don't talk to each other about it. What's there to say? Every Sunday they don't break up feels like a gift, like a little extra time the four of us get to share.

But finally, Break-Up Sunday arrives. They sit next to each other in our booth at Surf City Waffle but don't touch at all.

It happens just the way I saw in my vision. It's like having a movie-length déjà vu.

After Cassidy leaves, Sophie cries for an hour. She tells us that things have been bad between them for a while. She says it's like Cassidy had gotten bored with her. She did careless things, like forget when they had a date. Whenever Sophie complained, Cassidy told her she was too sensitive.

Martin and I hug her and let her cry until she stops. She tells us she doesn't think she wants to go on the road trip. I'm disappointed all over again, but then I let it go.

Later, after I get home, I call Cassidy and listen to her side of the story. Surprisingly, it's kind of the same. She says she thinks maybe she isn't a good girlfriend for anyone yet.

The next Sunday, Martin and I go to Surf City Waffle alone, but it's just too sad. We leave and go back to my house. I make us peanut butter and jelly sandwiches. We eat outside on the patio.

Mom starts seeing Dr. Bob twice a week instead of just once. I want to tell her not to put herself out there again. Doesn't she remember how she felt after Dad left? Doesn't she remember taking down their wedding photos? Right after he moved out, we tried living in our house for a few months. I'd catch her staring at the places Dad's stuff used to be. One toothbrush next to the sink instead of two. Empty spaces on the bookshelf, like missing teeth. The house became a museum of all the places love used to be. A few months later, she agreed to sell the house and we moved.

———

It's been twenty-one days since I found out that the boy I love is going to die. I want to say that every passing day is better than the one before, but it's not true.

There are places my mind refuses to go. Exactly when does he die, and how? I remember my vision of Archibald and Maggie standing in an open field, snowflakes drifting in the air around them, watching a coffin being lowered into the ground. How will they survive the death of their grandson? How will his parents? Kevin and Jamal and all his other friends? Will he know it's going to happen? Will he suffer? What will his last thought be?

Sometimes I want to call him and tell him the truth. But telling him would be cruel. Just because I'm burdened with this awful knowing doesn't mean he should be. I remember the round of Tipsy Philosophicals we played at our first bonfire, the one where we first kissed. I asked everyone if they'd want to know when and where we were going to die. X said no. He said it would take the fun out of everything. I said yes, that it was always good to be prepared.

Sometimes I want to call him and tell him the other truth, which is that I love him and I always will. But telling him that would also be cruel.

What would I say?

I love you, but you're going to die, so I can't love you?

I can't because I'm scared I won't survive the pain? Or, that's not right. I'm not scared I won't survive the pain. I'm scared the pain will never end and I'll have to live with it forever.

The problem with broken hearts isn't that they kill you. It's that they don't.

CHAPTER 55

The Fish and the Water

I'VE BEEN IN my room and in bed with the lights off for basically the entire weekend when Mom knocks on my door.

"Come bake with me," she says. "I'm making bread pudding." She's wearing her *Kiss the Cook* apron.

"I'm not really in the mood," I say, burying myself even farther under the blanket.

"Well, you're doing it anyway," she says, pulling my blanket off. I know from her tone that I don't have a choice.

As soon as I get downstairs, she points to the recipe and hands me a stack of measuring cups and spoons. "You do the dry ingredients."

I get the sugar and cinnamon from the pantry.

She waits until I'm busy cubing bread to say what she wants to say: "I want you to tell me what happened with you and X."

"I don't want to talk about it," I say. I grab another slice of bread and keep on cubing.

We're back to communicating in sighs. Hers now is Frustrated. "I'm your mother, and I know something happened. I don't understand why you won't talk to me."

All I want to do is go back to bed and pretend the world doesn't exist. "You first," I say.

She's been whisking eggs, but now she stops to look at me. "Me first what?"

"You want me to talk to you, but you never talk to me." I measure out the sugar and pour it into a bowl. "How many times have I tried to get you to talk to me about Dad?"

"This again?" she says, and restarts her whisking. "The business between me and your father is between me and your father."

I don't mean to cry, but tears are suddenly welling behind my eyes and in my throat, like they've always been there waiting. "You're not the only one Dad left. He left me and Dani too." I drop the measuring cup onto the counter. "He left us too."

The air between us is shocked. She looks stunned and then devastated. Her hand flutters to her hair and then to the whisk and back to her hair again. "Sweetheart," she says. She pushes the bowl away and pulls me into her arms. "Don't cry, sweetheart, don't cry."

I pull away from her. "Why does everyone keep telling me not to cry when there's plenty of things to cry about? Why do you and Dani act like everything is fine?"

She looks down at the counter, presses her fingers into it. "How do you want me to act?"

"I want you to stop pretending that everything isn't terrible now. Why aren't you angry with him? Why won't you talk about it?"

She sighs again, but this one isn't frustrated or angry. It's a release. "You want to know why I won't talk about it?"

I nod.

"Because mothers take care of their children, not the other way around. I wipe *your* tears. You're not supposed to wipe *mine.*"

She looks at me and her eyes are stark and filled with tears she won't let fall.

"I was devastated when your father told me what he was doing. I felt like someone reached into my chest and—" She stops herself and sucks in a breath. "Anyway. You think I wasn't angry with your father? I was angry. Sometimes I'm still angry." Her voice is soft, but the pain in it is loud, louder than it's ever been. "I didn't talk to you because I was trying to protect you. You and your father were so sweet together. I didn't want this thing to change the way you felt about him."

How have I managed to be so wrong?

I thought she wasn't feeling enough. It turns out she was feeling *everything.*

It turns out she was trying to protect me from all the everything she was feeling.

She looks at me again, and now she does let her tears fall. "Your father isn't the one who wanted the divorce. After he told me about Shirley, he said he wanted to stay together and go to counseling and try to work things out. I was the one who said no."

I'm so shocked my mouth actually drops open. All this time I thought Dad left us, but it was Mom. Mom did the leaving.

"But why?" I ask. "You loved him. You love him still."

"Yes, but I could see he loved her in a way he didn't love me anymore. I wasn't going to sit there being someone's runner-up."

I stare at her for a long time. I stare until I'm not just *looking* at her, I'm actually *seeing* her. I see my mom, strong and stoic and capable. I see my mom, soft, brave and vulnerable. Everyone says there's a moment in your life when your parent becomes more than just a parent and becomes a real person. They never said how scary that moment would be. And wonderful too.

"Can I ask you one more thing?" I say.

"Lord have mercy, please let this be the last of it," she says, but she's smiling.

"It's about Dr. Bob. After everything with Dad, how are you okay with dating again?"

She pulls the bowl of eggs back toward her and picks up the whisk. "Well, first of all, I like Dr. Bob. I like him a lot and he likes me a lot. But besides that, what else am I going to do? I can't just cut myself off from love. I'm not made that way."

"But look what happened with Dad. Look how it ended."

"You think because your father and I didn't last, our love was any less real? Once upon a time, your father and I loved each other enough to make you and your sister. That alone makes all the other nonsense worth it."

She cuts me a look that says she knows why I'm asking her about this. "I don't know what happened with you and X, but I hope you know you can't cut yourself off from love either."

"I'll be okay by myself," I insist.

She laughs at me. "You ever hear the one about the fish that didn't need water?"

"No," I say.

"Me neither," she says. She takes my dry ingredients and dumps them into the eggs and mixes them all together.

CHAPTER 56

Once and Again

GRADUATION IS A week later. Our valedictorian gives a speech using cheese as her primary metaphor. We started out as young, mild cheddar but have since aged into sharp, mature Gruyère. Even though some teachers and classes *grated,* high school was still a *Gouda* experience. She concludes that we're leaving stinky with knowledge.

Her name is Olivia Cortez, but I only know her by reputation—supersmart, sweet, destined to do something incredible, the same way Sophie is. I wish I'd gotten to know her.

After Olivia is done with her speech, Mr. Armstrong (history teacher extraordinaire) has his boring way with us one last time. He delivers a speech about the history of modern warfare as it relates to us making a place for ourselves in the world. He uses phrases like "behind enemy lines" and "in the trenches."

We all groan and wish for cheese.

Next, it's Principal Singh's turn. He tells us we have bright futures, because of course he does. Since our class is too big to bestow diplomas individually, he holds up an oversized symbolic diploma, presents it and declares us Bevshire High School graduates.

"Now go out and leave your mark on the world," he says.

After the applause dies down, I get up and go to find Martin.

"We made it," he says, as if he wasn't sure we were going to. He throws his arm around my shoulders and kisses the top of my head.

"Do you feel ready to make your mark on the world?" I ask.

"I don't want the world, Eves, just my piece of it."

I follow his gaze and find Danica at the end of it. He squeezes my shoulder. "Your sister's relationship status is single again," he says.

"Since when?"

"Last night."

"How often do you check her status?"

"Once a day or so. Is that stalking?"

"No."

"Are you sure?"

"No."

He lets go of my shoulder and turns to face me fully. "Are you still okay with me asking Danica out?" I know he's asking because of what happened with X and me.

"Yeah, I'm okay," I say. Still, I have to ask: "Are you sure you want to do this?"

"There's only ever been one thing on my graduation bucket list."

"And she's it?"

"She's it."

"What if she says no?"

"Then she says no." He ruffles his own hair. "But what if she says yes?"

I hope she says yes. I hope she doesn't break his heart, but it's his heart to break. As much as I'd like to, I can't protect the people I love from pain. And besides, Martin's braver than I am. He'll take the pain with the joy. He thinks it's worth it.

He kisses me on the forehead again. "Let's go find Sophie and Cassidy before our parents swoop in," he says.

We spot Cassidy standing by the stage scowling. Her parents are next to her, chatting up Principal Singh.

I overhear her mom thank him for all he's done for her little girl.

Cassidy scowls harder. Her mom has no idea if Principal Singh did anything at all for "her little girl."

Martin and I pull her into a hug a couple of feet away.

"They came," Martin says, meaning her parents.

Cassidy shrugs like it's no big deal, but I can see that she's relieved they're here. "They got in last night."

"I'm glad," I say, since she's not going to.

"They leave again in the morning," she says. Then she takes a deep breath. "I think I'm going to go with them. Japan, Korea, China. Might be fun," she says.

I smile too bright at her.

"I'm sorry about the road trip, Evie," she says. "I know how much you wanted to do that."

I wave her off. "Listen, I'd go to Asia with my superrich parents too."

We hug. I know it's the last time we'll be this way

together. When she gets back from Asia, she'll be different. We all will be.

We find Sophie surrounded by her parents and her sisters. She's holding a bouquet of pink roses and still wearing her graduation cap.

Just like we did with Cassidy, we abduct her for a hug.

"Can't believe this day is finally here," I say.

"Me neither," she says with a sniffle.

Martin hands her his handkerchief. "No crying," he says. "We still have summer."

She wipes her tears but then sniffles some more. "Olivia asked me out," she says.

"Our valedictorian Olivia?" Martin asks.

She nods. "Did you know she's going to Stanford too?"

We did not know that.

"And did you say yes?" I ask.

"Yup," she says with a small smile. She looks around the yard for a second and then turns back to us. "Did you guys see Cassidy?" she asks.

"Yeah. Her parents came," says Martin.

"That's good," she says.

I decide against telling her about Cassidy's trip to Asia. Their lives are separate now.

The three of us hug again. I wish Cassidy were here. I want one last Sunday at Surf City Waffle with the four of us. I want one more bonfire. One more Tipsy Philosophical.

But I can't have that. I think back to the day I made up with them at Cassidy's house. I remember how we hugged right before I left. We were all full of waffles and the sun was bright and we smelled like sunscreen and pool.

Mom said just because a thing ends doesn't make the thing any less real. Just because everything is different now doesn't mean we didn't love each other once. Maybe we will again.

CHAPTER 57

Two Dresses

DANICA KNOCKS ON my door the Friday night before Dad's wedding. She's holding two dresses. One is a simple lavender sheath trimmed with lace. The other is a complicated teal-blue-and-silver mermaidlike thing.

At first, I think she brought the lavender one for me, since it's my kind of dress. "Dani, I haven't changed my mind," I say.

"No, I want you to help me choose," she says.

I eye both dresses again, not sure why she's asking me to decide. Teal is her favorite color, and complicated is her favorite style.

I choose the teal one.

"Thanks," she says, and hangs the dresses on the back of my door. She sits down on the edge of my bed. I scoot over to give her more room.

"I broke up with Archer," she says.

She looks sad but not devastated. "How come?" I ask.

She gathers her hair into one hand and then lets it loose again. "It just wasn't that much fun anymore. Every time we were together, I just wanted to be with my other friends. I kinda think he felt the same way."

"I'm sorry," I say. And then I have a thought. "This might be too soon to ask . . . but how long do you think it'll take you to get over Archer?" I ask.

"A few days. Why?"

"You know my friend Martin?"

"Of course."

"He's liked you since the dawn of time."

"He has?"

"Come on, you must've seen the way he looks at you."

Her eyes are smiling. "I wasn't sure."

"You think he's cute," I say, taking a guess.

"I think he's . . . interesting," she says, with a grin. "I've never seen so much tweed on a teenage boy in my entire life."

I laugh and laugh. Of course she would notice the way he dresses.

"How come you never went for him?"

Her smile dims. "He's your friend. I didn't think you'd like it if we got together."

She's right. I wouldn't have liked it. I would've been afraid of what a relationship between them would mean for my friendship with Martin. We wouldn't be as close anymore. I'd be on the outside.

But as much as I want to, I can't stop the world from changing. Time passes. People change. Lives move on.

"I think you and Martin would be great together."

"Really?" she asks.

"Really, truly," I say.

She scoots closer and lays her head on my shoulder. Her hair tickles my nose. "Can I ask you something without you getting mad at me?" she asks.

"I can't predict the future," I say.

"Come on, promise me," she insists.

"Fine, fine, I promise."

"How come you changed your mind again about going to Dad's wedding?"

I don't have an answer for her, not really. The wedding just felt like too much, too many complicated emotions to deal with on top of everything that happened with X.

The last time I saw Dad was at graduation. Afterward he took me to Mariscos Chente for lunch. He decided our valedictorian was a genius and riffed on cheesy puns until my sides hurt from laughing too much. He even managed to combine a Mexican-food pun with a cheese one.

Q: *Why should you always bring a bag of tortilla chips to a party?*

A: *In queso emergency.*

He didn't ask me again to go to the wedding and he didn't call me sweet pea. For the first time I saw what our relationship could be like at some point in the future.

Danica picks her head up from my shoulder. "At least tell me why you're so mad at him. Is it only because he left?" she whispers.

"What do you mean?"

She stares at me for a long time, scared of something. "You don't think he and Shirley got together before—"

I know what she's asking. She's asking if he had an affair. I think about what knowing the truth has done to me. I think of what it would do to Danica.

Some illusions don't need shattering.

I shake my head and hold her eyes. I am completely and totally convincing. "No way," I say. "Dad would never do that."

Her relief is acute, and I feel like a good big sister.

"You should come to the wedding," she says again.

"Why?"

"Because he's our dad and he loves us and he's getting married to someone he loves and we should celebrate that with him."

It's so simple for her.

"Also, it'll be easier if we do it together," she says.

I look up at her and understand that this whole thing has been harder for her than I realized.

"Okay," I say. "But I don't have a dress."

"How about that one?" she says pointing to the lavender one, the one I liked better.

I shake my head. "You didn't need my help choosing a dress at all, did you?"

"Nope."

"Your plan when you came in here was to get me to go to the wedding, wasn't it?"

She laughs an evil laugh and tumbles off the bed before I can catch her. "Yup," she says.

"Okay," I say once I've stopped laughing. "Okay, I'll go."

CHAPTER 58

Answers

I WAKE UP the next morning knowing I have apologies to make. I ride my bike over to the studio and haul it—one last time—to the top of the stairs. Fifi is in the reception booth, explaining something about how to sign clients up for lessons to a woman sitting at the computer.

As soon as she sees me, her eyes go wide and then narrow again. "Oh, look who it is. The vanishing dancing queen." She quick-steps it out of the booth, stops about a foot away from me and folds her arms. "Did not think I would see you again." She's not just being her usual Fifi self. I hurt her feelings.

I take a step toward her. "Fi, I'm sorry for running off and for not calling and for not saying thank you. I'm really sorry."

She sniffs and taps her heels and considers. "Not nice to abandon people who care about you," she says.

"I know. I'm really sorry, Fi," I say again.

Finally, she smiles. "I'm glad to see you. Will not ask why you ran away from dance like girl who lost shoe in fairy tale," she says.

By "will not ask" she means she's about to ask me.

Lucky for me, Archibald and Maggie come gliding down the hallway.

"Well, isn't this a wonderful surprise," Maggie says, wrapping me in her rose-garden hug. "Has Fifi filled you in on all the wonderful things that have happened?"

"Most important news is that we hire real receptionist," Fifi says, pointing her thumb at the woman in the reception booth. "Already, I throw away infernal *ding-ding-ding*," she says, jabbing at her own hand to demonstrate how the desk bell worked.

Archibald laughs. "Fortunately, that's not the only good news," he says. I forgot just how much his eyes twinkle when he talks. "Enrollment is up forty percent since Danceball. Next week *LA Weekly* is sending a reporter to do a photo shoot and an interview."

"That's incredible," I say, and I mean it. It's great to hear that something good came out of this experience.

"It's all thanks to you, dear," Maggie says. She means thanks to me and X, of course, but she's too considerate to mention it. I wonder what X has told her about our breakup.

We talk for a little while about my plans for the rest of summer and NYU in the fall. I promise to stop by to visit before I leave and to find a place to keep dancing in New York. And then it's time for me to go.

Archibald and Maggie hug me one more time before going back into the heart of the studio. Impulsively, I hug Fifi, and she surprises me by hugging me back and holding on tight. "You are very good dancer," she whispers into my ear. "I was proud to teach you." I can't prove it, but I swear I see something like tears in her eyes when she pulls away.

Just as I'm about to leave, I spot the *Instructions for Dancing* book sitting in the back corner of the reception booth, where Fifi tossed it the first time I came here.

My heart trips. I know it's not a coincidence that I'm seeing the book right now. I know I'm supposed to see it.

"Hey, Fi, can I take that book?" I ask, pointing at it.

She gets it and hands it to me through the reception window. "Of course," she says, "but is very silly. Cannot learn to dance from a book."

"I know, but it led me here, right?" I flip to the page with the La Brea Dance address on it. It seems like a lifetime ago that I walked in here hoping I was going to learn whatever lesson I needed to learn to get rid of the visions. The Evie that walked in here that day thought she understood how unfair life could be, and how painful. That Evie had absolutely no idea.

I put the book into my backpack and take one last look around. Down the hallway, in front of studio five, I see Archibald pull Maggie into a twirl. At first I think that they have no idea how lucky they are. But then I study the look on both their faces, a combination of wonder and certainty, and I know I'm wrong. They know exactly how lucky they are.

———

It takes me barely any time at all to get to the Hancock Park neighborhood. The street, when I find it, is still overflowing with jasmine bushes and jacaranda trees. The Little Free Library is still next to the big sycamore tree.

I get off my bike, flip down the kickstand and walk over

to the library. All my books, including *Cupcakes and Kisses,* are still inside. The memory of X texting me as he read it makes me want to laugh and also to never laugh again.

I take *Instructions for Dancing* out of my backpack and stuff it inside.

"Hello, Evie," says a voice from behind me.

I never told her my name, but really, how she knows my name is the least mysterious thing to happen to me in months.

I whirl around. Her face is the same as I remember: weathered brown paper.

"Why did you do this to me? How did you expect me to feel, watching people get their hearts broken over and over again?"

She smiles at me. It's a gentle smile, an understanding one.

I don't know if a smile has ever made me angrier.

I'm mad at her for cursing me with this terrible power.

I'm mad at whatever force created a world where we are born to love and also to watch the people we love die.

People who say it's better to have loved and lost than never to have loved at all have never really loved anyone and never really lost anyone either.

I want answers. I want to know—I want her to tell me— how I'm supposed to live without my heart inside my body.

My anger leaves me all at once. I just want to know why. "Why did you give me the power to see heartbreak? Please tell me."

"But that's not the power I gave you," she says.

"What, then?"

"I gave you the power to see love. The heartbreak is just one part of it. It's not the all of it. Why did you only focus on the ending?"

"Because it's the most important part."

"Is it?" she asks. "It wasn't supposed to be a curse, Evie. It was supposed to be a gift."

I start to cry and I'm sure that I will never stop. When I come back to myself, she's still standing next to me.

"Will the visions go away?"

"Yes," she says.

"When?" I ask, even though I know she won't give me a straight answer.

"When you're ready."

I get on my bike.

"Take care of yourself, Evie," she says as I ride away. And just like the first time, when I get to the end of the street and turn to look, she's no longer there.

Dad's wedding doesn't start for another three hours. I wander through the streets on my bike. There are fewer petals on the jacaranda trees and jasmine bushes. The wet green smell of spring has been replaced by summer's bright and smoky one.

I don't know how long I ride around, only that it's more time than I think it is, and less too. I keep hearing the old woman's voice in my head.

It wasn't supposed to be a curse.

I think back to all the visions I've seen.

There's more love in each and every one than there is heartbreak.

When I get home, Danica does my makeup and lends me a chunky vintage necklace to go with the lavender dress. We

kiss Mom goodbye and tell her we love her. She promises me she's okay.

In the cab, I squeeze Danica's hand. "I'm glad we're doing this together," I tell her.

"Me too," she says.

CHAPTER 59

Do Us Part

AT THE CHURCH, it's almost embarrassing how happy Dad is to see me.

More sweet than embarrassing, though.

He picks me up and spins me around. "I'm so thrilled you're here, sweet pea." He puts me back down. "Sorry, I keep forgetting not to—"

"No, it's okay. You can call me that."

He closes his eyes and drops his head. For a second it looks like he's praying. He pulls me into another hug and squeezes tight. I squeeze him right back.

"Group hug," yells Danica, who's been hovering in the doorway.

By the time we're done hugging, all three of us are a mess of tears.

Dani grabs my chin in one hand and clucks at me. We find a bathroom, and she pulls a mini emergency makeup kit from her purse. She operates on herself before operating on me. I check the mirror once she's done. She's a miracle worker. I am saved.

By the time we make it out to where everyone is, the pastor is already at the altar. We take our seats next to Aunt Collette.

And then it's time.

The music begins. Dad walks up the aisle and takes his place in front of the pastor. His best man, Uncle Allan, and Shirley's maid of honor are next. Then it's Shirley's mom, walking by herself. Next it's Shirley's bridesmaids, all ten of them. Once everyone is settled at the altar, the music stops.

Dad stares down the aisle, waiting.

Uncle Allan squeezes his shoulder.

Another few seconds pass before the wedding march begins. Everyone turns to look.

Except me. I watch Dad's face instead. I don't need to see Shirley to know when she's arrived. I can see her presence on Dad's face. He looks like someone who just can't believe his luck.

Shirley reaches the altar and takes Dad's hand. She looks beautiful. And also like a tiered cake.

As weddings go, this one is pretty traditional. The vows are the normal ones. They promise to love and obey. They promise to do it forever. There are some readings. Shirley's mom sings a gospel song I don't know. Her voice is beautiful.

The priest pronounces them man and wife. He tells Dad that he may kiss the bride.

I have a few seconds to decide.

I can choose to see their future.

I can choose to see how it ends, and maybe even when.

But at the last second, I close my eyes.

I close my eyes, and I pretend they have forever.

———

The reception is in a hotel ballroom twenty minutes away. Dani and I take the wedding shuttle together, along with Aunt Collette and Uncle Allan. I drink sparkling cider, eat hors d'oeuvres and listen to Dani critique the dresses of all the women in a kind way. She tells me the history of marriage as an institution. Mostly it sucked for women.

After a while, the wedding band gets everyone's attention. "Ladies and gentlemen, please welcome Mr. and Mrs. Larry Thomas."

I have a moment where my heart breaks for Mom, the original Mrs. Thomas. But then I remember that she did what was best for everyone, including herself.

And then everyone is clapping and hooting.

Shirley is crying and Dad is wiping her tears. He tells her that he loves her and that he always will.

All that matters is that he feels it now.

All that matters is right now.

I turn to Dani. "I have to go," I say.

———

In romance books there's always a chase scene. It happens near the end, when one person realizes they've made a colossal mis-

276

take and then has to go through a series of obstacles to get back to the other person.

My chase scene starts just outside the hotel, where there is a line of cabs waiting. It's only after I get into one that I realize I don't know X's address. I text Fifi. Miraculously, she's not teaching a class. She texts me Archibald and Maggie's address right away. She can't resist adding:

don't know what took you so long
boy is too sexy to let go of
good luck

Traffic getting back to LA is awful because . . . because traffic in LA is always awful. It takes us forty-five minutes to get to midcity. The cabdriver turns onto Wilshire. Unbelievably, traffic is even worse. It'd be faster for me to ride my bike. I tell the driver to turn onto Curson and take me to my apartment instead. I run inside and grab my bike lock key. I don't stop to change my clothes. I can bike in a dress. By the time I realize I'm still wearing my heels, I don't have the patience to go back. All I can think of is getting to X as soon as possible. There are so many things to say to him and not enough time to say them. I don't want to miss another second of being with him.

I hear the old woman's voice in my head, telling me that the power would leave me when I was ready. And I feel the moment when it does go away. Weirdly, it's like adjusting the focus on a set of binoculars. The power leaves me, and the world is somehow clearer than it was before.

Maggie answers the door when I get to her house. She looks like she was expecting me and gives me a hug. "You look very nice, dear," she says, before telling me that X is playing guitar in the living room.

The very short walk from her door to the living room is the longest I've ever taken.

I don't know exactly when or how X is going to die. I don't know how I'm going to survive the crater he'll leave inside me.

The only thing I know for sure is that I can't live with knowing I could've had more time with him and I didn't take it. It doesn't matter that love ends. It just matters that there's love.

X stops playing as soon as I'm in the doorway, as if he can sense me there.

"It's my dad's wedding today," I say.

He stares down at his feet. "When?"

"Right now. I mean, it happened already."

"Did you go?"

"I did. It was nice. The reception is happening right now."

He looks over at me. His eyes are sad and wary, but at least they're on me. "Why are you here, Evie?"

"I need a dance partner."

"You came all the way over here in the middle of your dad's wedding to ask me to dance with you?"

"Yes." I leave the doorway and sit next to him on the sofa.

He hugs his guitar tighter and shifts slightly away from me. "I don't know, Evie. You messed me up pretty bad."

God, I've wasted so much time already.

"I know," I say. I reach out and rest my hand on his shoulder. He doesn't flinch, so I keep going. "I'm sorry. I was scared."

"Of what?" he asks.

"Of losing you."

278

He hangs his head down, not looking at me. "You don't make sense. You're scared of losing me, so you dump me?"

"It seemed safer."

"You were never going to lose me," he says, frustrated. "I tried to tell you."

I stand up and pace a little, trying to find the right words. "I'm screwing this up. What I'm saying is I finally figured out that endings don't matter nearly as much as I thought they did."

"What matters, then?"

I sit back down. "Beginnings are nice, but the best part is right now, in the wide-open middle. I made fun of you, but you were right this whole time. I should live in the moment and all that other stuff."

He lifts his head and turns to face me.

Now I know the right words to say. "You're the love of my life, Xavier Darius Woods. I've never loved anyone as much as I love you."

His smile starts off small just at the corners of his mouth before spreading to take over his entire face. "I'm the love of your life?" he asks.

"You are. It's terrifying, frankly."

He laughs at that and then bumps his shoulder into mine. "You're the love of mine too, you know."

"I know," I say.

He stands and tugs me up with him. "So you want to go dancing at your dad's wedding?"

"I do. Will you go with me?"

He grins. "I ever tell you about my philosophy of saying yes to everything?"

CHAPTER 60

The Future

WHEN WE GET to the reception, the lights are dim except for a giant disco ball spinning silver light. The band is playing, and most everyone is dancing. Dad and Shirley are in the center of the floor. I think they're doing the (slow, boring, English) waltz, but it's hard to tell because they're pretty terrible dancers. What they lack in skill, though, they make up for in happiness.

I look around for Danica and find her eating cake and talking to someone on the phone. I wonder if it's Martin. I hope it is.

The song winds down, and I pull X along with me so I can ask the band to play an Argentine tango. Lucky for me, they know how.

At first, I'm self-conscious. I notice the way everyone notices us. I notice them studying our dance moves. After a while, I don't notice anything but X.

Eight months from now, X will be playing guitar at home in Lake Elizabeth. He'll feel a pain in his chest. Afterward, doctors will determine that he had a bad valve in his heart and that he'd had it since birth.

By then, we'll have written an entire album together.

We'll have danced for hours and hours.

We'll have made love.

He'll have taught me how to play guitar and to love music as much as he does.

He'll have told me that he loves me every single day.

Some days I'll know that I'll be okay. Some days I won't know that at all.

One thing I'll know for sure: love can last forever.

Now, he spins me around. My arm travels down the length of his. Our fingertips brush and it feels like I'm going to slip away from him.

But I don't.

At the last second I curl my fingers and our hands catch.

And then I do the thing you're supposed to do when you find love.

I hold on.

ACKNOWLEDGMENTS

A few disclaimers before I begin: I'm sorry to say there's no such thing as Taco Night in Los Angeles. There very definitely should be, but, alas. As is my right as a writer of fiction, I also took some liberties with the structure of ballroom dance competitions. Also, Barrington, New York, is not a real place. Neither is La Brea Dance. Surf City Waffle does not exist, but it's based (loosely) on my favorite waffle place in all of Los Angeles, called Met Her at a Bar. It's delicious and you should go there. If you do, say hi to Vinny and Mindy and tell them that Nicola sent you.

I wrote this book during one of the hardest times in my life. My mom was very sick. For more than a year and a half, we weren't sure if she would make it. My father-in-law was told he had a terminal illness. He died a year later. If you've ever cared for a seriously ill or grieving loved one, you know what this is. You know how illness and death remakes the world. At the very least, it introduces you to a shadow world, one made of endless doctor's visits and of 3:00 a.m. phone calls followed by lonely 3:05 a.m. drives to the hospital. You know what it is to hold someone in your arms and make promises you don't know if you can keep. And promises you absolutely know you cannot.

Throughout this process—this remaking of my world—I wrote. Writing has always saved me, and I thought it would again. Most of what I wrote during this time was not good. In particular, I wrote a book (the never-to-be-published precursor to this one) that was just okay. I rewrote it for a while, but it was not meant to be. I wrote a lot of other things that were also not meant to be. It turns out I couldn't *write* my way through this period—I could only *live* my way through it. Finally, two and half years after the publication of my previous book, I started on the one you're holding in your hands. I've never fought harder for a book, and I'm very proud of it.

And now for the part that always makes me cry as I write it:

Thanks to every nurse, doctor, security guard, janitor, parking lot attendant, receptionist, every everybody who helps take care of the sick and dying. Thanks for being kind to a lost and grieving daughter and daughter-in-law.

Thanks to my teams at Alloy Entertainment and Random House Children's books: John Adamo, Shameiza Ally, Josh Bank, Matt Bloomgarden, Emily Bruce, Ken Crossland, Elysa Dutton, Colleen Fellingham, Felicia Frazier, Gina Girolamo, Becky Green, Romy Golan, Judith Haut, Beverly Horowitz, Alison Impey, Christina Jeffries, Kimberly Langus, Wendy Loggia, Barbara Marcus, Les Morgenstern, Amy Myer, Alison Romig, Mark Santella, Tamar Schwartz, Tim Terhune, Adrienne Waintraub and publicist extraordinaire Jillian Vandall. Thanks also to Judy Bass and my indefatigable agent, Jodi Reamer. You guys are rock stars, and nothing happens without you.

An extra-special shout-out to my editor, Wendy Loggia, for being patient and kind on top of everything else she is. Another special shout-out to Martha Rago and Neil Swaab for the gorgeous cover design, Jyotirmayee Patra for the lovely hand lettering and Renike for the stunning illustration. And still more extra-special shout-outs to Joelle Hobeika and Sara Shandler, who believed in me and believed in me and believed in me when I didn't believe in myself.

During times of stress, I tend to retreat from the world. The hugest of thank-yous to David Jung and Sabaa Tahir, who made me talk when all I wanted to do was hide. I love you guys a lot.

Thanks to my mom and dad and sister and niece just for being.

Thanks to my little girl, Penny, for noticing the way rain changes the colors of the world. You are pure magic and I love being your mama.

And, finally, thanks to my husband, David Yoon. I'm the luckiest because I get to adventure through this life with you. I love you forever.

Don't miss the #1 *New York Times* bestseller that everyone, everyone fell in love with.

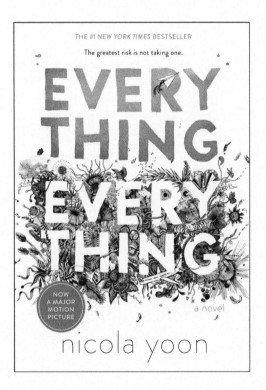

Best Book of the Year: *Bustle* • *Huffington Post* • *PopCrush* • *Booklist* • *The Miami Herald* • *SLJ* • The New York Public Library

Now a major motion picture!

Don't miss

THE SUN IS ALSO A STAR

#1 *New York Times* bestseller, a National Book Award Finalist, a
Michael L. Printz Honor Book, and recipient of
multiple rave reviews, including six starred reviews.

Now a major motion picture!

ABOUT THE AUTHOR

Nicola Yoon is the author of the #1 *New York Times* bestsellers *The Sun Is Also a Star* and *Everything, Everything,* both of which have been turned into major motion pictures. She grew up in Jamaica and Brooklyn and lives in Los Angeles with her husband, novelist David Yoon, and their daughter. She's also a hopeless romantic who firmly believes that you can fall in love in an instant and that it can last forever.